BILLY

A Tale Of Terror

By

Clayton E. Spriggs

This book is a work of fiction. Names, places, characters, events, and situations in this book are purely fictitious. Any similarity to actual persons, living or dead, is entirely coincidental.

Copyright © 2015 Clayton E. Spriggs
All Rights Reserved.

No part of this book may be reproduced, or stored in a retrieval system, or transmitted in any form or by any means, electronic, mechanical, photocopying, recording, or otherwise, without the express written permission of the publisher.

Published by Penn Mill Publishing.
Slidell, Louisiana
www.pennmillpub.com

ISBN: 978-1-945842-89-4

For Jennifer,
my beautiful Cajun queen

Man is the cruelest animal.

       Friedrich Nietzsche

PART ONE

THE ST. PIERRES

CLAYTON E. SPRIGGS

Chapter One

Bebette

"Don't just stand dere, *couyon*. Get some water berling!"

Dorcelia St. Pierre didn't suffer fools, even when the offending party was her husband. She could see her daughter was in agony, and the dimwitted patriarch of the family was doing nothing but getting in the way.

"You watch how you talk to me, woman. I'll not be trifled with in my own house."

The big, ugly oaf shot his wife a dangerous look that she understood too well. Dorcelia knew her husband was cruel and could be violent when provoked, but she'd had enough. It was beyond repulsive what the sick bastard had done to his own daughter. He'd brought them this shame, but the girl was in a perilous state.

"Ooooooohhh! Aaaaaagh!" the child

shrieked in agony as she writhed in pain on the sweat-soaked sheets.

Her cries echoed off the bare cypress walls in the confined space of the back bedroom, competing with the clamor of the rainstorm that rumbled against the tin roof overhead.

"You need to go get Doc Besson before sumptin' bad happens," Dorcelia implored her husband in vain.

She knew the old fool wouldn't budge. He'd embarrassed the family with his unspeakable sin, and he'd do everything in his power to distance himself from the crime. Even the life of his only daughter didn't hold much weight against his misguided sense of pride and instinct for self-preservation.

"You know 'taint happenin', woman," Poppie belligerently replied. "De rain be comin' down strong for hours now. No way to get help now even if I were inclined to do so."

Poppie St. Pierre knew his wife well enough to know she was all talk. She stood silently by when he did those regretful things in a drunken, lustful state, and she now shared in the guilt. It was the girl's own mother that forbade any discussion of the matter, as if silence might retroactively undo the transgression or prevent its reoccurrence. She'd been proven wrong on both counts.

"Eeeeeehhh!" the girl screamed between

BILLY

labored breaths.

"Dis be on your head, *capon*!" Dorcelia spat back at her husband as she turned to tend to her afflicted child.

"You shut dat door. *Fait pas une esquandal!* You slow down dat racket," Poppie shouted as he turned his back on the women with righteous indignation.

How dare she call him a coward under the roof he provided for her comfort! Damn woman's got a slappin' comin' her way, he thought, as he walked away and unsuccessfully attempted to put his daughter's screams of agony out of his mind.

Dorcelia slammed the wooden door at her husband's back and tended to her daughter's needs. She was no midwife, but she'd had enough children of her own to guide her. Dorcelia took her daughter's hand, feeling the child's grip squeeze tightly. With her free hand she stroked the sweat from the girl's forehead and tried to soothe her as best she could.

"Dere, dere, *cher*, shhhhh. It's gonna be alright. Momma's here."

"I'm scared, Momma," the girl cried.

"I know, Lillian. You gonna be fine. Jus' listen to me and do da best you can, and I'll pull you tru dis."

The girl nodded and started to breathe heavily as the torturous clawing in her gut resumed. Dorcelia pried her hand free of her daughter's grip and positioned herself at the foot of the bed in preparation for the imminent arrival of the family's newest member. She could see that her daughter was close now, and Dorcelia found herself as afraid as her daughter. She hid her feelings for the sake of her frightened child and swallowed hard.

"It's almost time, *cher*. You gonna have to push when I tell you and breathe when I tell you. It's gonna hurt sometin' awful, I ain't gonna lie to ya, but you gonna get tru it, I promise."

"Aaaaaaahhhhhh!" Lillian screamed and twisted on the bed as the baby inside of her tried to push itself out of her womb and into the waiting arms of a cruel world.

"Ooooooooowwwww!"

"Push! Push!"

"Eeeeeeehhhhhh!"

"Breathe now, child."

Dorcelia could see that Lillian was ignoring her instructions. The girl's face was turning red from the exertion as she bore down trying to expel the offending item from her body and the agonizing pain with it.

"Breathe, Lillian, breathe!"

A splatter of blood sprayed into Dorcelia's face, and she recoiled in disgust. Peering down between her daughter's legs, she saw

BILLY

the baby's head emerge with force, then its slippery shoulders coming out one at a time. Dorcelia took a deep breath and grabbed hold of the newborn to help guide it out.

She almost dropped the child in horror when it suddenly pushed out on its own in a violent fury, ripping a ragged gash in its mother's body and spraying more blood around the room in its wake. Suppressing the sensation of nausea, Dorcelia held onto the wriggling baby in her arms and glanced at her silent daughter.

"*Oo ye yi*!" Dorcelia cried.

Lillian's face was forever frozen in agony, the last sensation she was to know in her short, sad life. The girl's eyes stared blankly toward the heavens, while her limp body lay in a pool of blood on the dirty sheets. Her once ruddy complexion was now a ghostly white, contrasting with the blue lips of her repulsive grin.

Dorcelia's tears ran down her face as she cried in silence, her voice not able to reach the depth of her mourning. The wriggling ball of flesh in her arms broke her trance, and she looked down at the baby she held. The child was covered in blood and amniotic fluid. Dorcelia grabbed the cleanest piece of cloth near her and began to wipe away the sticky mess and inspect the newborn. She could tell right away something was horribly wrong as she peered down into the baby's face.

"Bwwaaa aaa aaa!" the infant cried, spitting saliva and more blood into Dorcelia's face.

Dorcelia retched with disgust at the sight of the deformed baby in her arms. Its eyes were a reddish color, reminding Dorcelia of the blood that surrounded her. The baby's face was misshapen, and it resembled one of the vile creatures that inhabited the swamp more than it did a human being. His hips and legs were out of place, resembling those of a frog. The webbing between the baby's toes and its thick, discolored skin added to the child's reptilian appearance. She counted six claw-like fingers and toes on each of the revolting beast's appendages. The devoutly Catholic woman took that as a confirmation of God's condemnation of her husband's unforgivable sin and her own apathy to her only daughter's plight.

"My God, woman!" Poppie exclaimed as he burst through the door. "What is dat terrible noise? You scaring da chirren."

Poppie froze in horror at the unexpected sight before him. His daughter's contorted body lay lifeless on the blood-soaked sheets, and the vision of his wife reluctantly cradling what appeared to be nothing short of a monster in her outstretched arms made him

BILLY

stop short.

"*Qui c'est q'ca*? What is dat?"

"Dis be your doin', *Grand Beede*. God has sent his judgment for your sin."

"*Oo ye yi*! It be a little monster. A *bebette*!" Poppie exclaimed with shame and horror.

He glanced toward the lifeless body of his daughter stretched out on the bed. "Lillian, what you done to us, *peeshwank*?"

"Don't be blamin' da girl or da baby. It your doin'. You be da only monster here," Dorcelia replied accusingly.

"Bwaaa waaaa bwaaa," the newborn cried.

Poppie was at a loss for words. He looked down at the deformed creature in his wife's arms with disgust before turning away in silence.

He knew his wife was right. The creature was a curse from God for his unspeakable sin. He refused to acknowledge that it was merely a baby. If he admitted that to himself, he would be forced to concede that it was his child. He was the monster's father.

No, he refused to do that. It wasn't a baby at all; it was a curse. It was an unholy creature, a demon child, a little monster. The Cajuns had a name for such a beast — *bebette*.

CLAYTON E. SPRIGGS

Chapter Two

Billy

"Bwaaaa baaa aaa," the infant cried, its mournful screams ignored by the others in the small cabin.

"I can't take dat caterwaulin' no more," Poppie shouted above the din.

Dorcelia turned from her household duties and reluctantly walked over to the crying child. Once in her arms, the baby's screams became less fierce as he pressed his misshapen face into his grandmother's chest. Dorcelia never quite got over her feelings of disgust at the child's distorted appearance, but she suppressed her misgivings for the sake of her family's tranquility.

Ever since the boy's birth and his mother's subsequent demise, turmoil had reigned in the household. The child's beastly appearance only heightened his unwelcome arrival into the family. His very presence was believed to be a punishment from God for the sins that created him.

The boy's mother, only a child herself, had not survived long enough to witness what she had wrought. Dorcelia was eternally grateful her daughter had been spared this knowledge. She felt that the girl had already suffered enough in her short life.

"Bwaaa baaa aaa," the infant's pitiful cries echoed around the room.

"That *bebette* sounds like da Devil himself," Poppie continued in his rant. "Should've buried him with his mama."

"*Mais, jamais d'la vie*! Don't you ever talk about my poor child like dat again, you *bon rien*!" Dorcelia shot back. "Dat *peeshwank* done no t'ing wrong. It was you brought shame on us. Now my beautiful baby girl lay hidden in dem swamps forever, wit' no one to know she ever lived."

"She better off and you know it, woman!" Poppie shot back at his increasingly belligerent wife. "She played a part in dat shame, same as you. Don't be playin' all holy now, *bonne a rienne*. Girl in a better place now; no one gonna find her where she at. At least she can rest in peace, not like da rest of us with that demon child at our feet."

BILLY

"Bwaaa baaa baaa!" the little child screamed in response to the increasing tension around him.

"It sounds like a goat," Justin interjected in an attempt to disrupt his parents' ensuing melee.

"A demented, evil goat," T-Roy added with a grin.

Justin and T-Roy were the remaining children in the St. Pierre household. T-Roy was the oldest and the most like his daddy. A bully in the making and ignorant to boot, T-Roy idolized the patriarch of the clan and showed every indication of becoming just like him. Once grown, it was assumed he would have a swamp cabin of his own tucked away amongst the cypress trees, complete with a wife and offspring he could abuse to his heart's content.

Justin was the younger of the two and kept quiet most of the time, with the rare exceptions when he should have remained silent the most.

The two brothers performed their sadistic father's every command without question. This included wrapping the bloody corpse of their older sister in an old sheet and assisting in her secret burial deep in the swamp.

The burial place was as secluded as could be — a creepy location only fit for demonic spirits and ghostly entities that haunt the netherworld. An old, overgrown plantation that had sunk into the surrounding marshland long before the Civil War, *Lost Bayou Plantation* was almost unrecognizable as a man-made structure after being swallowed up by the stagnant waters and ravaged by the relentless passage of time. It was doubtful even the few inhabitants of the secluded region knew of its existence, which made it the perfect place to bury the family's deepest and darkest secrets.

To the few outsiders who knew of Lillian's existence, her absence could be explained without further inquiry. The entire clan refused to discuss it, with the only exception being a vague suggestion of sinful promiscuity on the girl's part and subsequent banishment to live with distant relatives. Of course, these insinuations only fueled rumors of an unwanted pregnancy and involvement with an unnamed male companion, with whom she'd run off. The silence about the girl's whereabouts that the St. Pierre household practiced surely pointed to a shameful outcome and successfully squashed anyone from pressing the matter further.

"Bwaaaa aaaa aaaa!"

"*Oooo yee*! Shut dat t'ing up!" Poppie started in again. "It gives me da *freesons*."

BILLY

"*Zeerahb*, that t'ing is disgusting," T-Roy added.

"He's not a t'ing; he's a child," Dorcelia corrected them. "Your child, *bon rien*."

"You watch now, woman, before I pass a slap at your sassy mouth," Poppie spat back at his wife. "It's not a child; it a monster — spawn of Satan. I make no claim to it. You listen to me. We need to put it out in da swamp and let da Devil take it back to da hell it come from."

"You do no t'ing of the kind. God himself pass punishment on da lot of us for Lillian. We gonna bear dis cross, or He doom us all forever to dat hell you goin' on about."

"We end up in dat hell already wit dat t'ing here. It gonna grow and den what? Little monster gonna be a big monster, and we all gonna regret it."

"Bwaaaa aaaa aaaaa!"

"Ech! Dat goat child give me da *mal au couer!* I'm gonna 'tro up," T-Roy joked.

"Dat 'goat child' is your brother, T," Dorcelia turned her gaze to her eldest.

"It ain't no St. Pierre," Poppie exclaimed. "I ain't givin' dat t'ing my name."

"It ain't got a name at all," Justin observed.

"It ain't an 'it'; it's a 'he'. And he gettin' a name, or I's namin' him after you," Dorcelia looked directly at her husband.

"*Beck moi tchew*, kiss my ass, woman! You ain't givin' it my name. You must be *bracque*!"

"Baaaaa aaaa aaaa!"

"Sounds like a goat ta me. We should name dat t'ing Billy," said T-Roy.

"*Ga-lee*! Billy it 'tis," Poppie laughed, pleased with the joke.

Dorcelia fumed, but kept quiet. Even a name given in jest was better than no name at all. Billy wasn't so bad. She could accept that. A name meant recognition. With a name, the child was no longer a thing, but a person.

Dorcelia knew that the child would never be accepted into the family. He was a symbol of their shame, an unwelcome entity to be hidden from the world. That part would be easy. No one outside of the immediate family knew of the child's existence, and as much as they all could help it, no one ever would.

There was no certificate of birth for the child, just as there was no acknowledgment of death for his mother. The sad, little, unwanted creature would be banished from the outside world and forced to grow up surrounded by those who despised him. But, if Dorcelia had anything to do with it, he would at least have a chance to live. It was a chance denied to her own daughter by her father's perversion and her own apathy.

BILLY

Dorcelia believed it to be their only chance at redemption and salvation, and she was determined to see it through.

"Bwaaaa aaaaa aaaa!"

"It's okay, *p'tit boug*. It gonna be alright," Dorcelia whispered to the distraught child in her arms. "You be strong, little one. Celia's gonna make sure Billy gets his chance one day."

She rocked the sobbing infant until his cries faded, and he drifted off to sleep. The little boy was disgusting to look at, she conceded, but he needed her more than ever. Dorcelia's resolve to protect the child from the abuse he was sure to be subjected to would never waver, even if, deep inside, she wondered if her good-for-nothing husband's dire predictions might have merit.

As if Poppie could read his wife's thoughts, he muttered once more, just loud enough for her to hear, "You let dat t'ing grow up, we all gonna regret it one day."

CLAYTON E. SPRIGGS

Chapter Three

Caimon Grand Papere

The St. Pierres played their cards close to their vests. They only ran into their scarce neighbors on occasion and almost never at their own home. The cabin in which they lived sat on wooden pilings long driven into the murky waters that surrounded them. They lived without a telephone and without electricity. A small hand-cranked pump supplied them with the only water supply not teaming with vermin, both seen and unseen. There was some muddy ground scattered about their property, though even this was generally only accessible when the water level was cooperating.

Privacy was assured by the sheer remoteness of the location, the camouflage of moss-covered cypress trees surrounding them, and the large population of dangerous predators lurking about.

The family possessed two *pirogues*, which are best described as small, wooden, canoe-like boats popular with the Cajuns who inhabit the vast wetlands of southern Louisiana. An old, rusted airboat was at their disposal – at least when it was working. More often than not it wasn't. An automobile was a luxury the family couldn't afford and had no real use for, since the only way to get anywhere near their home was with both a boat and a keen sense of direction.

Any potential visitors to the St. Pierre home better have an invitation if they valued their lives. The entire family was heavily armed and had no qualms about using their weapons under any circumstances. There were reasons they lived apart from the world around them, reasons they preferred to keep to themselves. The Landry family was the closest thing they had to neighbors, and even they were skittish about encroaching on the St. Pierre clan unnecessarily.

Jean and Earline Landry had three children – Luann, the eldest and only girl, and Robert and Tre, her younger brothers. In comparison to their reclusive neighbors, the Landrys were a little better off and

BILLY

considerably more sociable. They lived on a patch of solid land, enjoyed the benefits of electricity and telecommunications, and possessed an automobile along with the obligatory watercraft.

Earline was the closest thing that Dorcelia had to a friend and the only access the St. Pierres had to the outside world. It was Earline that ensured that Jean would ferry them over to St. Gabriel's for Sunday Mass and assist in acquiring whatever supplies they could manage to pick up in town.

It was common for the Landrys to quietly contribute toward their neighbor's necessities since what little Dorcelia brought with her was never quite enough to acquire even the most basic of supplies. The St. Pierres had no knowledge of the costs of things in the world around them, but would have baulked at the very thought of charity. The entire clan, Dorcelia included, would have preferred starvation over charity, and the Landry family kept to themselves what assistance they provided.

Years had passed since Lillian died and little Billy entered their lives. His father remained cruel and hostile toward him, berating him at every opportunity and kicking him as a habit when he was underfoot. His brothers taunted him unmercifully and terrorized him for their own sadistic amusement, much to the approval of their heartless father. It was only his grandmother who showed him any kindness at all, and even this was lacking in enthusiasm.

Billy was a cross for her to bear, a penance that she was burdened with for her family's wicked ways. Billy was a reminder of the family's shame. Billy was told over and over again who and what he was. He was told by his father and he was told by his brothers. Even the only person in the world that showed him any kindness told him without using any words at all just what he was. Billy was a monster.

His unsettling appearance increased in severity as he grew. His malformed face gave him a menacing look. Dark red eyes, glowing with an internal fire as if from the pit of Hell itself, gazed out at the world from the shadows of prominent brows. The rest of his face was relatively flat, the bottom half dominated by a wide mouth that bore jagged, pointed teeth reminiscent of the nocturnal predators that lurked under the swamp waters that surrounded them.

Billy's arms were muscular and, even at a young age, his upper torso gained an almost unnatural strength. His chest was wide and his lungs were able to hold enough air to allow him to stay underwater and

BILLY

undetected for endless minutes. Each of his hands had six long, thick fingers with nails ending in sharp points, making his grasp nearly impossible to escape.

Although his legs were almost frog-like in form and curved so much that they often appeared folded underneath him, they were powerful. His wide feet looked even wider because each had six webbed toes that ended in claw-like points, enabling him to both swim and climb through the soft marshlands at an alarming speed. His unkempt hair and skin looked almost like scales; dried mud and Spanish moss clung to his matted hair, camouflaging his presence in the dense foliage of his environment.

Shunned by his father and siblings, Billy was often forced to fend for himself. When he was six years old, T-Roy pushed him head-first into the murky water of the *bayou* in an attempt to drown him. Billy quickly learned how to swim. When he was eight years old, his father and two brothers left him behind on a small patch of ground just before sunset. The water rose around him and Billy taught himself how to use his claw-like hands and feet to scramble up into the trees.

He found that his beady red eyes that gave him so much trouble seeing in the blinding glare of the sunlight endowed him with superior vision in the dark. By sunrise, he was sitting on the front porch of the family home, much to the dismay of Poppie and the boys.

When Billy reached the age of twelve, his family began to grow frightened of him. His awkward movements developed into a cat-like agility that enabled him to move silently with a speed that even the hardiest of swamp predators would envy. Eventually, even Dorcelia relented to her husband's wishes and looked the other way once again as Poppie sought to inflict unspeakable evil upon his own blood.

"T-Roy, Justin, y'all come on now. We got gator huntin' to do," Poppie shouted to his two boys as he loaded up the airboat for the upcoming trip. "Billy, you wanna come wit us? Might learn a t'ing or two 'bout catchin' a real monster."

Poppie laughed at his own cleverness, while the two boys grinned. Billy peered at the three indecisively for a few moments, sensing another round of abuse that was sure to come his way.

"Come on now; no trick dis time. We goin' down da *bayou* after *Caimon Grand Papere*."

The legendary *Caimon Grand Papere* was the biggest, baddest alligator anyone had ever seen. He lived in a notoriously dangerous patch of marshland amongst a sizable congregation of gators that anyone

BILLY

without a death wish avoided at all costs.

The very mention of their destination almost made Billy's brothers abandon the venture, but they were as afraid of their malevolent father as they were of the beast they were going to hunt.

Billy sensed his brothers' fear and relished it. Fear was a sensation he had long since abandoned, and he forgot what it felt like to be scared. He did, however, learn to smell fear on his prey, usually right before the kill.

The enjoyment of filling his empty belly followed when he was victorious in the hunt, and he unconscientiously trained himself to associate the terror of his quarry at the prospect of its imminent death with the enjoyment of extending his own life.

Billy scampered over toward the three and climbed silently into the boat. He watched with curiosity as the others gathered the materials necessary for the expedition. He recognized his father's shotgun and T-Roy's handgun, though these instruments held little interest for him. Billy preferred to hunt his prey up close. The giant metal hook fascinated him. It was fastened to a steel cable that was coiled up on the deck. He surmised that bait would be attached to the line to lure the gators up close, then the guns would be utilized for the kill. Alligator skin was notoriously thick, and a beast the size of old *Caimon Grand Papere* would not go down easily.

Even at Billy's young age, he had become a master of the hunt. His inability to feel fear, coupled with a lack of nutrition, motivated him to great lengths in search of food. He watched the creatures around him and learned their secrets. Billy's hands were big and strong for his size; the extra fingers and sharp claw-like nails allowed him to seize prey and inflict his will upon it. Every kind of animal became his quarry – fish, turtles, snakes, birds, rabbits, nutria, and the like – met their fate as Billy's meals. It was only the alligator and the bear that he had avoided. He longed to conquer the challenge that these ferocious predators presented. Then there would be only one remaining foe left for him to vanquish.

Poppie fired up the engine, and the giant fan behind them began to spin. The noise was incredibly loud, but the sheer euphoria Billy felt when they took off temporarily distracted him from any other sensation. The wind pushed against his face, and he beamed with the unexpected delight inherent with his first experience of speed. He grinned with pleasure and his teeth, which he had filed into sharp points, gleamed in the bright sunlight.

Justin and T-Roy shivered at the sight of

BILLY

their deformed brother's appearance. To them, Billy looked more like one of the alligators they were hunting than a member of their own family. Poppie felt disgust at the repugnant image of the thing in his boat. He longed for the ride back later in the day without the hideous ogre at their side.

"We gettin' close now, boys," Poppie shouted out as he cut the motor and the boat drifted up to a quiet spot amongst the reeds and cypress knees jutting up from the water's surface. "Justin, you watch for dem *boscoyo*. We don't want a hole in da boat."

Poppie didn't have to repeat himself; Justin and T-Roy quickly scanned the water for the scattered cypress knots. The thought of being stranded without their boat terrified the two boys, particularly in the vicinity of *Caimon Grand Papere*'s lair. Billy shrugged indifferently to the possibility. His red eyes squinted in the daylight, and he searched for any sight of the legendary beast.

Poppie opened a box filled with rotten fish and began to bait the giant metal hook in preparation for the hunt. The stench of the rotting bait caused Billy's older brothers to gag, a sensation that was unknown to him. He smiled at the displeasure the putrid smell caused his siblings. Justin retched at the sight of Billy's grotesque grin, fighting with all of his might to keep from spilling what was left of his breakfast at their feet. His badly deformed brother made him *fremeers*, grossed out. Billy grunted in recognition of his brother's attention, a sound that disgusted Justin as much as the display of jagged teeth frightened him.

"Dat over dere is da gator pond," Poppie whispered, pointing to a green pool of stagnant water on the other side of a small patch of ground. "Y'all be quiet now, and we'll tie off to dat cypress tree over dere."

They drifted up and T-Roy tossed a rope around the moss-laden tree, then the four sat quietly awhile and waited. The boys occasionally swatted at the swarm of mosquitoes that harassed them while Billy ignored them completely, transfixed by the beauty of the deadly reptiles in the brackish water nearby.

Poppie crept up to the front of the boat and swung the giant hook, letting it go in an attempt to land it in the pond across the embankment. His motion proved strangely awkward, and the hook landed in the mud and out of range of the waiting alligators.

"*Maudit*! Goddamn it, missed by a long shot," he cried out in frustration as he tried in vain to retrieve the hook. "It's stuck on da *boscoyo* on dat other side. T-Roy, go unhook it, boy."

"No way, Poppie. You *bracque* if you 't'ink

BILLY

I'm goin' over dere."

"Don't you sass me, boy. You do as I say."

"Justin, you do it. I ain't 'bout to climb out of dis boat," T-Roy suggested.

"*Embrasse mon tcheue*! Kiss my ass! No way I's goin' out dere," Justin replied.

Without a word, Billy climbed out of the boat and scampered through the mud to unloosen the hook. He watched with fascination as the gators pretended not to see him and slyly drifted up closer to his position in preparation to attack. He freed the hook just in time and turned back toward the boat as the motor roared to life. He stared in disbelief as the men in his family smiled and mockingly waved goodbye. Poppie kicked the fan up full blast, and the boat shot out of sight within minutes.

Billy turned back to the approaching predators in time to see the legendary *Caimon Grand Papere* bearing down on him, mouth agape. The ferocity of the beast amazed the boy, and he could smell the foul odor of death from the creature's gaping jaws before his reflexes kicked in and he swung sideways, causing the gator to miss. The reptile's powerful jaws snapped shut with a loud pop and, before the giant beast could recover, Billy thrust the sharp end of the metal hook through the animal's eye and straight down into his skull. The alligator thrashed wildly about, but Billy was already safely out of reach in one of the nearby cypress trees.

Caimon Grand Papere pushed his enormous body back into the pond and rolled, trying desperately to free himself from the vile hook embedded in his skull. He became entangled in the steel cable attached to the hook and quickly found that he was terminally trapped in the metal web. The multitude of hungry alligators he shared the pond with pounced on the helpless prey, tearing into its flesh with reckless abandon.

Billy watched from above with glee as the reptiles fought for the tasty morsels of raw meat. He knew that a new pecking order emerged that day in the alligator pond. At the top, safely perched in the branches overhead, a new king reigned supreme – a boy with a hungry stomach and no fear. Below, his minions fought their own battles for their place in the cruel hierarchy. *Caimon Grand Papere* was no more. The king was dead; long live the king.

Chapter Four

Possede'

Poppie and the boys were pleased with themselves upon arrival back at the house that evening. Though they had found little in the way of food, their mission had been accomplished when they left the beast behind. Dorcelia grumbled underneath her breath, feigning outrage at the men's actions, but they knew even she was relieved at Billy's absence. No one said a word about the missing child through their sparse meal. None of them had any intention of ever mentioning his name again if they could help it.

By nightfall, the boys readied themselves for bed as their mother quietly performed her daily devotions to Jesus. Poppie lazily rocked in his chair, occasionally drawing a puff of low-grade tobacco smoke from his pipe.

"Eeeeeeeaaaaaaaggghhhh!"

The ghastly howl of an unknown predator echoed through the darkness of the swamp, causing the hair on the back of Poppie's neck to stand at attention. Dorcelia paused in her prayers and looked at Poppie, who had stopped rocking in his chair.

"What da hell was dat?" T-Roy asked with fear.

"You watch dat language, T," Dorcelia chastised her eldest son out of habit, wondering the same thing.

"Shhhh! Y'all hush now. I'm tryin' to listen," Poppie said. He put his pipe down on the table beside his chair, then stood up and slowly walked over toward the window.

The swamp was quiet outside their cabin. Whatever made that horrific noise temporarily silenced the creatures of the marsh.

"I don't hear nothin' now," Justin whispered.

Poppie held a finger to his lips and glanced around the room. They remained silent and strained their ears to discern the source of their fear. The wind occasionally blew against the netting and fishing gear outside, creating a melodic chime-like jingling, accompanied by the soothing

BILLY

rhythm of the tide against the pilings on which their house stood.

"Well, whatever it be, it's gone now," Poppie proclaimed.

They let out a collective sigh of relief and tried to resume their previous state of comfort, without much success. Dorcelia briefly resumed her mantra before her eyes popped open with panic once again.

"Shhhhhh!" she whispered. "I hear a scratchin' out front."

The family held their breath and listened intently. Dorcelia was right. The unmistakable sound of claws against wood made its way across their porch and directly to their front door. Poppie reached for his shotgun and slowly crept toward the door, preparing to greet their uninvited guest. He motioned for T-Roy, who positioned himself to the side, and reached over to open the door. A knock shot out of the silence and startled the clan, causing Dorcelia to shriek and Poppie to almost fire off a round.

"Whew eeee! You put dat gun down, *cher*, 'fore you shoot someone," Dorcelia instructed her husband. "Ain't no gator gonna come knockin' at da door, *couyon*!"

Poppie pointed the barrel down and took a deep breath before motioning for T-Roy to answer the door. When it swung open, they were greeted by the dreadful sight of Billy's red eyes gazing back at them, burning with hatred.

"*Maudit*! Goddamn! How da hell?" T-Roy exclaimed with surprise.

Poppie pulled up the barrel of his Mossberg and fired. Much to his dismay, Dorcelia was already at his side and yanked hard at her husband's arm, causing his shot to miss. Poppie, Dorcelia, T-Roy, and Justin were in a state of shock. Their senses were overwhelmed by the blast of the shotgun and smell of gunpowder in the tiny room, coupled with disgust and fear at the monster's unexpected return.

Billy showed no reaction to the commotion. He just stared at the lot of them for a moment before pushing past them on all fours and creeping into the house to share the comforts of home with his unloving family.

The tension in the house began to swell. It was clear to all of them that Billy was growing fast and out of their control. He was nowhere near the idiot they'd assumed he was. Although he never spoke, they could see that he understood them better than they'd thought him capable of. Billy was getting stronger by the day, smarter by the minute, and consequently, more dangerous. Even Dorcelia began to fear the boy, yet she still refused to allow Poppie to kill him outright.

BILLY

For the time being, all they could do was to give Billy a wide berth and keep a watchful eye on the beast.

One day, when the St. Pierres travelled into town for supplies and Sunday mass, they heard the story of the missing pipeline worker. One of the Exxon crew was doing some routine inspections deep in the marshland when he disappeared. Sheriff Galliano was asking everybody if they might have any ideas as to the man's whereabouts, but no one knew anything.

One of the deputies requested that the St. Pierres keep an eye out since they lived the furthest out in the swamp and knew it better than most. Poppie assured the deputy that he would do whatever he could, though he doubted the man could have survived long on his own in the hostile environment. It was understood by all that they'd most likely be on the lookout for what was left of the man's corpse, but this unpleasant fact remained unspoken in the presence of the women and children.

When the family arrived back at *Bayou Noir*, they couldn't shake the feeling that Billy had something to do with the missing oil worker. The boy often went absent for days at a time while hunting for prey deep in the swamp. He rarely looked hungry anymore, so it was apparent that his hunts were successful. When Billy was seen in the possession of a mysterious flashlight one day, the family decided that something had to be done.

"You see dat torch he's got?" Poppie asked Dorcelia. "It's got dat Exxon logo on da' side."

"Dat don't mean nothin'," Dorcelia answered. "He might have found dat t'ing floatin' around."

"He might have, but didn't, and you know it, woman." Poppie continued. "You see dat chain 'round his neck. It got gator teeth, bear claws, and you know as well as I some other kind of bones we know didn't come from no animal. He killed dat man out dere, and he gonna get around to us one day, if we let him."

"What you want me to say, *Vieux*? *Mal pris*, we stuck in a bad way," Dorcelia answered. "He's your *boug*, not just some wild beast."

"My foot, he's not! He's not just some misbehavin' child, *Boo*, he *possedé* if one ever was. He possessed," Poppie stated. "You say he not just some wild beast, but he ain't human, either."

"He's our punishment for what you done; for what we done," Dorcelia countered.

"And what about dat line man? Who gonna answer for dat?" Poppie asked.

"I don't know, *cher*. Maybe we gotta do

BILLY

some t'ing, but we can't just kill him," Dorcelia said.

"For true! Don't know if we even can. More likely, he get da better of us now," said Poppie. "But we gotta do somet'ing, and we gotta do it quick."

CLAYTON E. SPRIGGS

Chapter Five

Nine-One-One

"Nine-one-one, how may I help you?"

"Yeah, I'm calling to report something I found in the marsh."

Manny's phone crackled and popped like an old phonograph that was playing a worn-out and often abused record from the distant past. He knew the reception was always spotty at best out here in God's country, and he didn't want to lose the signal before he could complete the message.

"Please state your name and location, sir."

"My name is Manny Duplantis, and I'm out in the swamp off Bayou Pigeon Road."

The woman's voice on the other end sputtered in and out, and Manny knew that the operator probably had as much difficulty hearing him as he had understanding her.

"Damn Cingular!" he muttered with disgust and sighed in frustration.

Manny had trouble getting a quality signal out in the swamp regardless of the carrier he used, but he had to direct his anger somewhere. It had been a long day. Once the unintelligible ramblings from the operator subsided, Manny figured that it was his turn to respond. Taking a big breath, he tried again.

"I am off Bayou Pigeon Road. My name is Manny Duplantis, and I work for Louisiana Gas."

He paused to see if the voice on the other end successfully received his communication.

"Yes, sir, Mr. Duplantis. How may I help you today?" the serious, but pleasantly feminine, voice responded in a brief moment of clear reception.

Manny tried to picture the disembodied voice on the other end and could only come up with a young, college-age hottie in scant lingerie sporting an ample bosom and pouty lips. He knew that his prediction was probably one hundred and eighty degrees off, but, when afforded the opportunity, Manny always preferred to envision his female associates in the same manner. *I really need to get a hobby*, he thought to himself before returning his focus to the task at hand.

BILLY

"Like I said, I think I saw something floating in the marsh."

"What did you see, Mr. Duplantis?"

"It looked like a person; well, a body, at least."

The unexpected sight had been quite disturbing. Manny was trying to wrap things up for the day and get out of the desolate area before nightfall when he spotted the object. He figured that he would've missed it altogether if he hadn't been forced to stop to inspect his tires after running over a wayward alligator corpse on his way up the *bayou*. His tires proved to be in satisfactory condition though his nerves were now a bit frayed.

Manny felt uncomfortable out in the swamp alone, even after all the years he had worked out there. The terrain was treacherous and the area filled with all kinds of nasty varmints that showed no fear of human encroachment. As far as the cold-blooded hunters of the swamp were concerned, the only thing Manny represented was lunch.

"Can you give me your exact location on Bayou Pigeon Road, sir?" the voice inquired, crackling again with the poor reception.

"No, ma'am, I can't. Just send someone down here. I am sure you won't miss me and my truck. And hurry please, it'll be dark soon."

Manny waited for a response, but none came. He realized that his call had been dropped and quickly tried to call back to no avail.

"Damn Cingular!" he cursed again. Lately, the phrase earned its place at the top of his swear list.

He did his best to be a good employee of Louisiana Gas as well as a fine, upstanding citizen, but hanging out in the Atchafalaya Basin after sundown was asking too much. Manny walked back to his truck and opened the door, tossing his useless cellular phone on the dashboard and taking a seat. He contemplated leaving a note at the site and heading toward civilization, but thought better of it, so he impatiently waited. A half-hour passed before he rethought his position. It was beginning to get dark, and he knew it would be difficult driving out on the narrow dirt road once night fell.

Manny decided that he would put a safety cone in the middle of the road and another one as close to the body as he could so that the authorities could retrieve it and do whatever it was that they did when unpleasant things like this occurred. Climbing out of his truck, he grabbed two of the orange cones from the back and walked to where he made the gruesome discovery.

BILLY

He set the first cone down unceremoniously in the middle of the shell road and carefully walked over to the edge of the marsh.

Manny scanned the brackish water, but couldn't see the offending object in the failing light.

"Just perfect," he muttered in frustration.

He briefly considered trekking back to the truck and grabbing his flashlight, but changed his mind. Instead, he carefully set the second cone down at his feet and began to turn around when he caught a movement out of the corner of his eye. Startled, he jumped and turned his head quickly, but nothing moved. Relieved, Manny let out a breath and chuckled nervously to himself. It was then that he spotted the object floating just under the surface of the murky water at his feet.

CLAYTON E. SPRIGGS

Chapter Six

Prey

"Ten-four, on my way," Dean uttered into his radio before returning the receiver to its perch on the dashboard.

Deputy Arceneaux drew the lucky straw on this assignment since he was closest to the reported location. He figured it was more than likely to be yet another bullshit call about a floating body that didn't pan out. At least, he hoped it would be. Every once in awhile, an occasional carcass would materialize out of the swamp, although the majority of these cases tended to be an accidental drowning devoid of criminal mischief. The end result was always the same for the first officer at the scene — endless paperwork.

CLAYTON E. SPRIGGS

There was no telling how many people disappeared in the swamp over the years. The Atchafalaya Basin is comprised of over a million acres of sparsely populated marshland prone to flooding and home to a vast array of wildlife, much of which is considerably inhospitable to human beings. People came up missing from time to time throughout the area, so it was only natural that one would be found every now and then.

The deputy hoped that it would turn out to be a false alarm. Many times, people found 'things' in the swamp they couldn't recognize. Much in the way one attributes unexplained lights in the sky to unidentified flying objects, floating objects in the dark, scary swamp are seen as dead human bodies. Sometimes these are indeed bodies, though rarely human. Of course, there are always the exceptions, thought Dean.

The deputy drove cautiously down Bayou Pigeon Road, keeping his eyes peeled. It was almost completely dark outside and, even with his headlights shining down the narrow road in front of him, the way was treacherous. He occasionally stopped and swung his spotlight around to get a glimpse into the wetlands on either side of the road, but only the gloomy darkness greeted him.

A green, glowing fog made his surroundings surreal, like something out of a

BILLY

bad horror movie. Even after a lifetime of living near the swamp, Dean always felt a chill run up his spine at the strange phenomenon. He learned long ago that it was a by-product of the large amount of methane gas produced by the decaying vegetation and putrid waters of which the swamp was comprised. Scientific explanations did little to quell the feelings of dread the spectacle caused in him, particularly when the explanations involved rotting dead things.

After inching his car around a deceased alligator, the deputy spotted a Louisiana Gas truck up the road. Just past the abandoned vehicle, he saw a solitary orange traffic cone perched in the center of the passageway. He pulled up alongside the gas truck and parked.

Deputy Arceneaux stepped out of his vehicle and shone his police-issued spotlight into the driver's side window. The truck was empty, so he crept up toward the traffic cone in the street. The deputy spotted another cone lying on its side at the side of the road, almost in the marsh. He cautiously approached the site, swinging his light slowly side-to-side in an attempt to examine his surroundings in the dark. The truck's inhabitant was nowhere in sight.

Dean looked at the fallen cone at his feet. He could see some tracks in the mud, but was unable to determine if they belonged to the missing workman or one of the unsavory denizens that inhabited the swamp. The deputy shone his flashlight over the water to see if anything lurked under the dark surface, but all was quiet. If it weren't for the truck and two cones, he might have passed the site up altogether.

"Weird," Dean whispered to himself in the dark.

He felt an uneasy sensation sweep over him and shuddered. For some reason, he had the disturbing feeling that something was watching him from the shadowy wetlands. The deputy backed away slowly and began to turn when he saw the unmistakable signs of something gone horribly wrong.

Blood was splattered on the reeds to the side of the road – a lot of it. Dean swallowed hard and shone his light back into the dark swamp beyond the Spanish moss hanging from the cypress trees that surrounded him. The blood trail disappeared into the mist toward the unseen eyes that he could feel peering at him from the blackness.

By the time the sun rose over the horizon, the entire area on Bayou Pigeon Road was alive with activity. The State Police, Search and Rescue Units, and even some boys from the Wildlife and Fisheries Division had descended on the desolate location to aid in

BILLY

the investigation, all under the watchful eye of Sheriff Bobby Galliano.

Just as Deputy Arceneaux had reported, an abandoned truck was found parked in the middle of the narrow roadway a few yards from an orange traffic cone standing tall in the middle of the road and another toward the edge of the marsh tipped on its side. Steps from the fallen cone, a blood trail led into the overgrown marsh at the edge of the roadway. No further signs of the missing man could be found.

The area was now partitioned off, and men were assigned to search different quadrants in the hope of picking up whatever trail they might find. By the amount of blood splattered along the roadside, it was doubtful to those present that they would find anything but a mangled corpse.

"Damndest thing ever," Galliano said to no one in particular. "Surely there must be something left of the poor bastard."

"That's what I was thinking," Dean agreed. "I got here pretty quick after the call came out. I'm sure whatever grabbed him took off in a hurry when I pulled up, thank God. Still, I don't see how there'd be no sign of the body."

Sheriff Galliano grunted and scanned the horizon. Some local fishermen had shown up and were carefully guiding their boats under the supervision of the Wildlife and Fisheries authorities. Many of the men were carrying long metal poles that they used to poke and prod around in the murky water, hoping to snag onto something and jar it loose toward the surface. Particular attention was paid to the immediate section of marsh covered in dried blood. Despite the dozens of men actively engaged in the task, no sign of the missing man could be found.

"Do you think we should find a few divers to go down and look?" asked one of the State Troopers.

Dean almost laughed at the absurd suggestion before catching himself and turning away. Galliano stared at the man with an expression that was a combination of amazement and contempt, shaking his head. A few of the local fishermen close enough to have heard the comment laughed and muttered a few choice comments in Cajun French under their breath.

"Be my guest," Galliano finally suggested, "if you think you gonna find someone dumb enough to do that. Course, I don't know how they gonna see anything in that filthy swampwater anyhow, but I'm sure you thought of that before you opened your mouth."

The trooper blushed with embarrassment

BILLY

and returned to the search with his head down and his eyes averted. Bobby hated being so hard on the man. After all, he was only there to help, but the last thing they all needed at this point was everyone jumping in with one ridiculous idea after another. It was becoming evident that their search was going to be in vain. The gas man was going to join the unfortunate oil worker on the list of missing persons that was beginning to grow.

Sheriff Galliano kept his concerns to himself, but he knew he was going to have to do something about the emerging situation soon. He was starting to have a bad feeling that this was only the beginning. There was something new going on deep in the swamp, some predator that was hungry and growing bolder, a predator that had an appetite for human flesh.

CLAYTON E. SPRIGGS

Chapter Seven

Attic

"Go on, now. Do as I say, boy," Poppie snapped.

"What if he wakes up?" Justin asked.

"Then get da hell out of da way and I'll blast 'em," Poppie answered. "He ain't gonna wake up no how, not after all dat tranquilizer I put in dat *gumbo*."

"Come on now, Jus. I ain't gonna be da only one gotta touch dat *zeerahb* t'ing," T-Roy shouted at his brother.

"Dat's enough out of you two! I got da gun on 'em, so's no worries. Just do as I say, and it be all over soon," Poppie instructed the boys.

The idea came to him out of desperation not long after the oil worker came up missing. Although the man was never found, the St. Pierre clan knew what happened only too well. The poor man got killed and eaten by the same creature that lived under their own roof.

Even Dorcelia understood that something drastic was going to have to be done, though the stubborn woman would never relent to having them do what was necessary. Poppie argued to no avail, but his wife never wavered. She didn't seem overjoyed at his proposal either; none of them did, but no one could offer up any viable alternatives.

There was only one solution left for them, only one place they could put the boy where he could cause no further mischief. At least they waited until Dorcelia was out of the house before setting their plan in motion.

The boys lumbered slowly as they carried their sleeping brother to the spot under the hole in the ceiling. They sat him down as gently as they could, trying desperately not to awaken the beast.

"How we gonna git him up dere?" asked T-Roy.

"Justin, go fetch da ladder," Poppie said.

"Ain't no way we gonna be able to carry him up no ladder..." T-Roy began before he felt the sharp slap of his father's hand across his cheek.

"Enough of dat back talk, *couyon*. I ain't

BILLY

no *bioque*!" Poppie snarled. "Go get da rope and dat pulley from 'round da back. And tell Justin to get dose chains when he finished wit dat ladder."

T-Roy and Justin did as they were told. Before long, they had the rope and pulley in place. T-Roy carefully threaded the rope around Billy's chest and tied it off, then the two boys scampered up the ladder to haul their heavy load up into the dark confines of the hot attic.

Poppie stood below, with one hand on his firearm, and carefully guided their quarry into the small opening as the boys pulled on the rope. Once Billy was in the attic, T-Roy and Justin lowered him to the dank wooden floor and tried to catch their breaths as Poppie climbed up to help secure the beast with the heavy iron chains.

"What you two jus' sittin' 'round for? Dere's work to do," Poppie admonished the boys.

"We jus' catching our breaths. Dat boy be heavy as *merde*," Justin answered.

"Dat's 'cause I was doin' all da work, *paresse*, lazy son of a bitch," T-Roy muttered.

The boys began to push and shove on one another before an unexpected sound made them stop dead in their tracks.

"Aaaa aaa aaa," Billy moaned.

Poppie cocked his gun and pointed it at

Billy. They all stood silently for a moment, staring at the poor child who lay still on the dusty wooden floor beside them.

"Sshhh," Poppie whispered. "We better get him chained 'fore he wakes up. Justin, T-Roy, pull him over dere by dat post, and we'll lock him up and get out of here."

The three of them worked quickly and quietly to secure the sleeping boy before he came to. Billy was beginning to move a bit and groan incoherently as the tranquilizers wore off. None of them wanted to be there when he woke up and found out the predicament he was in.

After they had their brother's chains secured to both his legs and the heavy wooden beam, the two boys grabbed the pulley and rope and quickly climbed down the ladder. Poppie handed his gun down to T-Roy and flashed his light once more in Billy's direction.

The hairs on his neck stood up when he spotted the beast's beady eyes staring back at him, burning red with hatred. Poppie shuddered, and then climbed down the ladder, pulling the square wooden door over the hole behind him, leaving his youngest son in the dark.

Poppie and the two boys stood in the living room of the small cabin and stared at the ceiling. They could hear the occasional

BILLY

clinking of chains as Billy moved around the small space overhead; then silence. Several moments passed before the men looked at each other and sighed with relief.

"See now, dat wasn't so bad, was it?" Poppie stated, satisfied with his idea and the apparent successful results.

"EEEEEEaaaaaaaaahhhhhhhh!!!!"

The blood curdling scream that echoed from above shook the walls and rattled the windows of the small, wooden shack.

"*Oo ye yi*! Dat give me da *freesons*!" T-Roy blurted, his voice shaking with fear.

"I got da *mal au couer*," Justin said and ran out the door before losing the contents of his stomach into the murky water out front.

"You two bunch of *capons*," Poppie stated. "Dat t'ing is chained up tight. I seen to it myself. I jus' hope he shuts up 'fore your momma come home. Goin' to get enough grief 'bout the situation as it is."

Crash! Bang! Crash! The booming sounds came thundering down from above, increasing in intensity and fury with each successive beat.

"He's goin' to tear down da whole cabin, lest he settle down," said T-Roy.

"EEEEEEEaaaaaaaagggggghhhh!!!"

"Don't you worry none," answered Poppie. "He goin' to calm down in a bit, once he sees he stuck."

CLAYTON E. SPRIGGS

Poppie hated the beast that he imprisoned up in the attic, but he learned to respect the child's resilience. Poppie learned all too well that the demon spawn that haunted his existence wasn't going to wallow in despair, or be done away with so easily. No matter what cruelty or danger life threw the boy's way, the little *bebette* managed not only to survive, but to master it. Poppie tried to explain this to his wife, but he lacked the vocabulary or communication skills to make his point understood.

Poppie St. Pierre knew that the monster was a punishment for his unspeakable sins. The beast was sent from hell to exact revenge on him for his actions and deliver justice for his forgotten daughter. In the end, Poppie realized he would have to kill the creature, or it would feast on them all. Unfortunately, there seemed to be no convincing his wife of the inevitability of the situation.

He couldn't understand why Dorcelia was so steadfast in her demands that the monster's life be spared. He knew she was as afraid of the thing as the rest of them. Secretly, Poppie believed that his wife recognized that Billy was going to slay them all one day, but accepted their fate, maybe even welcomed it as their only chance for eternal salvation. Poppie St. Pierre didn't

BILLY

hold out much hope for eternal salvation; he knew his soul was damned.

"EEEEEEEaaaaaaaaagggggghhhhhhh!!!"

"*Fils de putain*! Son of a bitch!" Poppie muttered to himself.

The unnatural sound of Billy's screams sent shivers down his spine. He didn't have to wait for eternity — Poppie was in hell already. The Devil was upstairs in his attic, for now. Every once in awhile, he knew he would have to go up there to feed and water it; Dorcelia would demand it. Poppie wasn't about to argue with her about it. He figured that the only thing worse than having to feed the beast was risking it starving up there.

If Billy got desperate enough, even those heavy chains weren't going to hold him. No, Poppie thought, he would give it just enough to survive, but not enough to grow strong. If they got lucky, maybe the thing would grow weak enough that he could kill it one day when Dorcelia wasn't around, and he'd do away with their curse once and for all. Until that time came, they would all have to wait it out.

"EEEEEEEaaaaaaaaagggggghhhh!!!"

T-Roy looked at Poppie, his eyes wide with fear. "I got da *faiblesse*, I'm gonna faint."

"Steady, T."

"I jus' hope we ain't gotta go up dere for anyt'ing."

CLAYTON E. SPRIGGS

"No reason to. No reason to ever go up dere again."

Chapter Eight

Wrath of God

By the time Dorcelia got home, Billy had settled down. The only indication that he was up in the attic came from the occasional rustling of chains they heard overhead. As long as Poppie put some water and food within reach of the lonely beast, all was well.

It was the one chore that Poppie hated beyond all else, but he resisted delegating it to others. He knew that one misstep and things could get ugly fast, and he didn't want to risk T-Roy or Justin's lives unnecessarily. It was his punishment to have to tend to the demon in the attic, and he performed it begrudgingly.

Besides having to carry the food and water bowls up there, he also had to bring the empty bowls back down. Along with these came the not-so-empty buckets of filth. Billy was a nasty creature who created gut-wrenching amounts of the foulest smelling refuse one could imagine. Every time Poppie found himself hauling another bucket of waste to the outhouse, he dreamed of the day he could kill the beast once and for all.

It won't be long now, he thought. The next chance he got when Dorcelia wasn't around, he was determined that it would be the last time any of them would have to deal with Billy again.

It was a hot summer that year, and the smell from the attic was rancid. By the end of August, the stench was unbearable throughout the small cabin. Flies swarmed incessantly around their house, crawling on every surface and making everyone miserable. Poppie and the boys complained relentlessly about the situation, but Dorcelia was unsympathetic to their plight.

"You t'ink you boys got it rough, I'm here all day and night," she replied when prompted.

"You right," Poppie would answer. "Maybe you need to go to town and pick us up some sweet-smelling candles or somet'ing to help rid us of 'dis stench. And get somet'ing to drive dese flies away 'fore I lose my mind."

Dorcelia could sense that her husband was

BILLY

trying to get her out of the house, and she had no problem figuring out why. She knew it was only a matter of time before she relented and allowed the man to do what was necessary, but she held out as long as she could. In her heart, she understood that it would be best for everyone, including the poor, unfortunate boy chained up in the attic, but it was hard for her to let go.

As terrifying as he was, Billy was the only thing Dorcelia had left of her long-lost Lillian. She mourned her poor baby girl and what her husband – what they all – had done to her. Once Billy was gone, there was nothing left on earth to bear witness that her child had ever existed. There was only an unmarked grave deep in the swamp by an old abandoned plantation that served as her eternal resting place.

There was little doubt in Dorcelia's mind that the eerie and remote location was inhabited by scores of restless souls that had suffered greatly in life and spent their eternities haunting the creepy swamp in search of their tormentors. Billy would soon take his place amongst them, and she lamented the fact that his soul was perhaps the most tormented of them all.

Dorcelia finally relented and made plans to go to town on the last Sunday of the month. Toward the end of the week, outside events undid her plans for good.

Poppie and the boys were out front, unloading some of their fishing gear from one of the *pirogues*, when they heard a boat approaching. Dorcelia stuck her head out the door at the unexpected and unwelcomed sound of uninvited guests arriving.

"You get back inside woman, and do it quick," Poppie commanded.

"What if Billy...," Justin began.

"Hush, now. Let's see what da commotion 'bout first," Poppie answered.

A boat came around the bend, within sight of the St. Pierre cabin. It was Jean Landry and his son, Robert. They cut the motor and drifted up slowly toward the house.

"Hey dere, neighbor," Jean called out, waving his arms.

The Landrys knew that their neighbors didn't like visitors, and they tried to avoid coming this far into the swamp even when invited. This time, they weren't invited, but the impending situation demanded that they forgo standard precautions and make an exception.

Poppie and the boys stared silently at their uninvited guests. None of them were smiling, and Poppie unconsciously toyed with his shotgun while watching the Landrys approach. Jean and his eldest boy looked cautiously at one another before Jean nodded

BILLY

for Robert to halt the boat so that they wouldn't drift too close.

"Sorry 'bout the intrusion, Poppie," Jean stated. "Dere's some news I gotta pass on. Sheriff himself goin' 'round gatherin' up da folks, but figured even him not gonna come way out here. I told him me and Robert here would come out personally and see to it ourselves. Storms a comin'. S'posed to be a big one – monster, dey say. Da authorities say everyone gotta get out now whilst dey can. Me and the family gonna get out ourselves dis time, and you know we not doing dat lightly. We offerin' to take you and yours, if you want. Christian t'ing to do and all."

T-Roy and Justin looked over at each other, not knowing what to think. Dorcelia stayed inside the cabin, unseen by Jean and his boy, afraid of what she knew her husband was going to say.

"Appreciate dat, Jean," Poppie answered. "But we be jus' fine. Ain't da first storm dat come dis way, and won't be da last. We never left before and don't see no reason to now."

"I figured as much," Jean replied. "But had to ask all the same. If'n you change your mind, you better do it quick. S'posed to be here by Sunday, and not much time left to get to higher ground."

"We ain't goin' to change our minds,"

Poppie said. "Y'all be careful out on da road, and tell dat sheriff don't waste his time comin' out here 'cause we ain't leavin'."

"Don't let dat worry you none, Poppie," Jean answered. "No one gonna come all da way out here now. Take care of da wife and dose boys, and tell 'Celia we sends our love. You'll be with us in our prayers."

Poppie nodded and watched as Jean and Robert started up their boat and rode out of sight. No one else was coming to *Bayou Noir* to warn them or see if they needed any help. There was not enough time now. It was almost Friday, and within two days, the storm would be upon them. Dorcelia wasn't going into town this weekend, and Billy was staying put. They were going to hunker down and ride out the hurricane for good or bad. Only then would they take care of the unsettled business in the attic.

For the remainder of that day and all of the next, they hurriedly prepared for the coming onslaught. The boats were double and tripled tied off to the dock, and as much of their possessions as possible were taken in to the relative safety of the small cabin. What they couldn't bring in, Poppie and the boys tied down as best they could. On Saturday night, the rain began to fall, and they shuttered up the windows before settling down together inside the wooden

BILLY

shack.

By the next morning, the wind began to howl. Strong gusts crashed against their home and shook the tiny building, only to be followed by an eerie silence uncommon so deep in the swamp. Generally, they were surrounded with a concert of the natural sounds emanating from the vast array of wildlife that lived in the marshlands. Not today. The swamp was quiet. The creatures that could leave had already left; the ones that could not were hiding from the upcoming melee, much like the St. Pierre's. The only other times Poppie remembered the swamp being this quiet was on the days when Billy was on the prowl.

Billy had been riding out the storm all alone in the dark attic in relative silence. The occasional sound of rattling chains drifted down from above to remind everyone that the monster was still waiting in the space above them, but no more noise than what they usually heard from him.

From time to time, Justin claimed to hear a creepy scratching sound and wondered aloud what the beast was up to, but no one else ever claimed to hear it. In these instances, T-Roy routinely mocked him, calling him a *capon*, which usually resulted in the two boys coming to blows before being forcefully separated by their irate father. By the time Poppie was finished with them, the damage they had inflicted upon each other paled in comparison. By the time that Sunday afternoon reached them, no one was calling anyone else a *capon*.

As darkness began to fall, the water began to rise. By this time, the wind was howling loudly – only now accompanied by Billy's howls from above.

"EEEEEEEaaaaaaaaaaaagggghhhhh!"

The waves crashed against the pilings on which their house stood, and the entire world swayed from the force of the hurricane. One of the shutters tore off from its mountings, and one of the window panes cracked from the power of the wind. A loud screech rang out as the wind and rain shot in through the small opening.

"Go get dat board and push it against dat window," Poppie shouted to T-Roy above the din.

"EEEEEEEeeeeeeaaaaaaaagggggghhhhh!"

"It's getting bad out dere, Daddy," Justin shouted. "What we gonna do?"

"We gonna be alright, Jus. We just sit tight and hold on."

"EEEEEeeeeeeeeaaaaaaggggghhhhhh!"

"*Maudit*! Goddamn!" T-Roy yelled. "Billy's going *motier foux*, half-crazy up dere."

The heavy chains rattled above in time with the thunderous clasps of the raging

BILLY

storm. The family below huddled in each other's arms at each crash of Katrina's fury.

"EEEEEeeeeeeaaaaaaaaagggghhhhh!"

"Ooo eee! Dat howlin' giving me da *freesons*," Justin hollered.

"Dat boy just scared, same as us," Dorcelia exclaimed.

"EEEeeeeeeeaaaaaagggggghhhh!"

"He ain't scared. Not dat one," answered Poppie.

He knew better. He had looked on as the beast confronted alligators and poisonous snakes raw-handed without hesitation, without fear. Hell, Poppie thought, almost with evil delight. He knew the demon he unleashed into the world wasn't human. Billy was the Devil himself. The monster didn't feel fear, except the fear in others, and at those times, he relished it.

"He up dere all alone, in da dark," Dorcelia pointed out. "Of course, he's scared."

"EEEEEeeeeeeeeeaaaaaagggggghhhh!"

"Dat don't sound like no fear to me," Poppie said. "Almost sound like he likin' it."

The family shuddered collectively at the thought. A loud crash hit the cabin and almost knocked them all down. The front door blew open from the force of the tidal surge. Cold water rushed in at an alarming rate. In seconds, it was up to their ankles; within minutes, up to their waists.

"Poppie," shouted Dorcelia, "what we gonna do?"

"Get dat ladder, T," Poppie shouted. "Jus, get my shotgun."

Dorcelia said nothing, tears running down her cheeks as she bit her tongue. Justin handed the gun to his father and helped T-Roy position the ladder under the small, square opening in the ceiling above. Poppie climbed up and pushed the wooden door open, then reached down to grab the flashlight from T-Roy. The water was climbing up toward their chests, and the entire family was beginning to panic.

"Hurry up, Daddy," Justin shouted, his voice cracking with fear. "We all gonna drown."

Poppie glanced at his boy, but said nothing. Justin was right. He had to do what he had to do. He took a deep breath, and then headed up the ladder.

He pushed his way quickly into the small opening and swung his light around. The rancid smell hit him, and he promptly choked back his nausea. A blast of cold water hit him in the face, the result of a hole that the storm had torn through the aged roof. Poppie felt the cold water at his feet and knew he had little time left before the entire family drowned. He flung himself up into the attic and leveled his shotgun, aiming for the

BILLY

spot against the far wall where he had chained his youngest child. He shone his light in the dark and froze in terror at the sight of empty chains.

Lightning burst through the ragged hole in the roof and lit up the dank chamber. The beast's shadow flashed upon the wall to Poppie's right, and he swung toward it and fired. The blast rang out in unison with the thunder clasp overhead and temporarily blinded him. He felt sick and heaved the remaining contents of his stomach onto the dirty floorboards in front of him.

"Daddy, please help us," he heard from below.

Poppie swung the flashlight around to the empty spot where he had fired his shotgun. Another flash exploded in the sky above the cabin and lit up the attic. Poppie swung around just in time to see Billy's sharp teeth inches from his face. The beast was laughing with sadistic pleasure, feeding off of the cruel man's fear at his impending death. Poppie looked into the dark red eyes of his son and breathed his last breath. Billy swung his sharpened claw with almost supernatural speed and ripped the old man's neck open, sending blood splattering out from the severed arteries and veins.

The water was up to their necks as the clan held on to the lone hope that their father's blast had cleared the attic of the waiting beast. Dorcelia stood on the table and clung to Justin as she craned her neck to keep above the rising tide. T-Roy stood on the ladder, almost to the top, as he waited for his father's call. They all heard the blast and held their breaths.

Another crash of thunder shook the cabin, followed by a brief moment of silence. A sickening thud echoed off of the ceiling and a trickle of blood dripped out from the attic opening and landed on T-Roy's face. He glanced toward his mother and brother, seeing the horror on their faces, then looked up again in time to see the square, wooden door to the attic slam shut on them, sealing their fates.

"EEEEEEEEEeeeeaaaaggggghhhhh!"

Within minutes, the water overtook them all. Dorcelia accepted her death as punishment for failing once again to protect her children from the evil under their own roof. Justin scratched and clawed at the ceiling above as water filled his lungs, feeling like the *capon* his brother branded him as his life gave way to darkness.

Even as his life slipped away, T-Roy never tried to gain access to the attic. The last thought in his dying brain was the realization that his father was right. The beast was savoring the moment. Billy's howls

BILLY

were not born of fear; they were roars of victory.

"EEEEEeeeeeeeaaaaaaggggghhhhh!"

The storm tore a hole in the roof of the small cabin and the rain poured in, riding on the gusts of the powerful wind. The sensation reminded Billy of the time he rode on the airboat, when the feeling of speed made him feel exhilarated. He was free of his chains, free of his prison in the attic, and free of his tormentors below. When the storm was over and the waters subsided, Billy stared out of the hole in the damaged roof and toward the endless swamp that surrounded him.

"EEEEEeeeeeeeeeaaaaaaahhhhhh!"

Freed from his chains by the storm, Billy was loose.

CLAYTON E. SPRIGGS

PART TWO

PRODIGAL SON

CLAYTON E. SPRIGGS

Chapter Nine

Evangeline Defante'

By the time Nick returned from the Search and Rescue Conference, everything had changed. His untimely departure from the Crescent City, prior to the horrendous events in the late summer of two thousand five, only exacerbated the alienation from his co-workers that he had already established. Timing is everything and, without it, Nick had managed to end up with nothing.

It was his decision to leave early for the meeting with the hope of escaping the oppressive summer heat of New Orleans. A couple of weeks in Colorado were just what he felt he needed to recuperate and recharge his system. Nick hoped that he'd be able to start fresh upon his return and eventually regain the respect and camaraderie of his fellow officers that he'd lost after his last assignment. No one liked anyone associated with the Internal Affairs Division, particularly an undercover operative, and Nick held out only a faint hope of recovering professionally from his ill-advised rotation. The fact that he was successful in his duties only made his fellow officers despise him more, and the chance of cooperation with any future endeavors harder to obtain.

Although Nick made every effort to return home after the levees broke and the city flooded, all that was remembered was that he was not there. By the time he reported back to duty, weeks had gone by and the National Guard was already in place. A large portion of the population had long since vacated, and groups from all over the country were providing the lion's share of the search for survivors and recovery of the deceased. His new position in Missing Persons was much needed, but not at all secured because of his absence when he might have been the most useful. Nicholas Vizier missed his chance of redemption once again. It wouldn't be the last time.

What was left of his home in the eastern part of the city was a heartbreaking sight. His humble abode was never all that much to begin with, little more than a two-bedroom

BILLY

single-family dwelling in a sketchy part of town that was well on its way to becoming a ghetto. Still, as humble as it was, it was all Nick had. Now, it was gone.

The waterline was clearly visible on the exterior wall at about ten feet high; the interior was a sad and putrid mix of mud, mold, and garbage. The stench was unbearable inside, even before he opened his refrigerator without thinking. Even the faintest of memories his olfactory nerves held of the event would continue to cause him to retch for years afterward. Judging by the multitude of discarded freezers taped shut at every curb, he figured he was not the only one to have made that mistake.

From that moment on, he wore a bandana soaked in cheap cologne around the bottom half of his face every time he ventured into the abandoned dwelling. Third world technology trumped first world luxuries in times of disaster, thought Nick. When he caught a glimpse of himself in the broken mirror above his bathroom sink, his reflection reminded him of a bank robber in some ridiculous B-movie Western. Drawing two pistols with his fingers and thumbs, he aimed and fired at his absurd image. Nick shook his head and chuckled, then tears welled up and drifted down his dirty cheeks, his sobs choked by the pungent cloth tied across his mouth.

Nothing in his house was salvageable. Nick sighed at the pathetic sight, thinking about the irony of it all. His domicile mirrored the state of his career. The wasteland that was his home symbolized his life. There was nothing left for him here; there was nothing left for him anywhere. It was time to go home.

Although he was born in St. Martinville, Nick spent his formative years moving from town to town every couple of years. His father, Russell Vizier, was a marginally-employed electrician and handyman who never seemed to have enough money or luck to support either him or his family. A raging alcoholic and habitual gambler, Nick's father moved his family from pillar to post in an unsuccessful attempt to gain steady employment and run from creditors.

When Nicholas was ten years old, his father left the house for a pack of cigarettes and never returned. Nick waited for his father on the front steps of the ramshackle duplex his family lived in at the time to no avail. His heart was broken at the realization that his father had abandoned him and his mother, and he longed for the day when he would see his father again, if only to repay the pain that he had felt. He never got his chance for revenge, however,

BILLY

since his father was never seen in the vicinity again.

His mother, Evangeline Theriot Vizier, wasn't nearly as heartbroken as her only son. She was pissed off. The sorry excuse for a man she had made the mistake of marrying was a poor provider, a terrible husband, a lousy lover, and an absent father. He left his own son waiting night after night for his return without so much as a goodbye. Once again, he left the dirty work to his wife. The family was already three months behind on the rent, and by this time, their landlord's patience had run out. Abandonment or not, eviction was inevitable.

Mrs. Vizier moved her and her son to a trailer park right outside of Plaquemine and managed to obtain work in a domestic capacity for one of the elderly ladies that lived up the road in an oversize plantation style home. She worked hard for long hours to give her son a stable environment at last. One of her proudest moments came when little Nicky was accepted into the Louisiana State University over in Baton Rouge. By this time, her poor child's heart had been broken a second time when his high school sweetheart ran off with his best friend; once again, he was abandoned without so much as a note.

Little Nicky had always been a misfit,

never quite fitting in, always an outsider. Evangeline hoped and prayed that he would find happiness in his new life, wherever that might lead him.

When Nicholas left after graduation to seek his fortune in the quagmire of New Orleans, Evangeline worried about her son. He pursued a career in law enforcement in a city that knew ugliness and violence in ways that the small towns she was accustomed to could not fathom. He visited only rarely, the memories of his painful childhood too strong for him to bear. Evangeline understood. When her friends and neighbors commented on how sad it was that he abandoned his mother, she remained silent and never took it to heart. They didn't know her son like she did. They could never understand what it was like for her son to never belong, to never have a real home.

When Nicholas arrived at the St. Gabriel Nursing Home, he learned once again the importance of timing. The staff quietly informed him of his mother's passing two months prior. They assured him that every attempt had been made to contact him, but with the arrival of the two hurricanes and their aftermath, no one was able to get in touch with him. Nick stopped listening to their feeble explanations. He just wanted to know where she was buried.

BILLY

He brought a small bouquet of fresh daisies, his mother's favorites, and placed them at the site where her remains were laid to rest. Only a small cement stone in a field of stones indicated that his only relative had ever existed. It dawned on Nicholas that when his turn came, there would be no one left to mourn his existence. He didn't care; there was nothing he had accomplished that warranted recognition, but his mother had been a saintly woman. She had given much more than she ever had received. She sacrificed her happiness and comfort for a husband who abused her and a son who abandoned her. He felt guilty for his shameful and selfish actions. He hoped that she understood how grateful he was for everything she had done for him and how much he had loved her.

"*Pauvre' Defante'* Evangeline," Nicholas whispered into the wind as tears rolled down his cheek. "My poor sainted mother."

CLAYTON E. SPRIGGS

Chapter Ten

Welcome Back

"Bobby's in the back. Just wait here a minute and I'll let him know you're here. Mr. Vincent?" the deputy asked.

"Vizier, Nicholas Vizier," Nick corrected the man before sitting down in one of the uncomfortable wooden chairs in the lobby.

Deputy Arceneaux disappeared into the back room of the Sheriff's Office for a few minutes and left Nick alone with his thoughts. He wasn't sure if this was a good move on his part as he was certain some of his ill-gained notoriety followed him. Lieutenant Foster called ahead and gave him a good recommendation, Nick was sure of it, but he knew that the sheriff would make a few calls of his own. Louisiana law enforcement was a close-knit community and word got around quickly, particularly when it came to 'rats'. Even so, Nicholas reasoned that no matter where he went, his reputation would follow him.

"Sheriff Galliano will see you now," the deputy called out, motioning toward the big office in the back.

Nick walked toward the sheriff's office, pretending not to notice the stares from the other officers who, in turn, were pretending not to stare. Bad acting seemed to be a prerequisite for small town policemen.

"Mr. Vizier, pleased to meet you," the sheriff said, extending his hand.

After their introductions were completed, the two sat down, Nicholas trying to appear relaxed while the sheriff glanced through some file or another.

"Lieutenant Foster called," Galliano said aloud. "He gave you a glowing recommendation."

Nick just nodded and remained silent. He knew what was coming next.

"Of course, I made a few calls of my own," the sheriff continued. "Doesn't look like you made many friends over in Orleans Parish."

"Internal Affairs never does, Sheriff," Nick answered.

"Nope, I don't suppose they do. All the same, I don't really think I have a need for

BILLY

any internal investigators at this time."

"I figured as much. That's not why I'm here. My specialty is missing persons. My stint in the rat patrol was done as a favor to the previous police chief. As you probably know, the NOPD has had numerous problems with corruption and unfit officers. When some of my fellow officers began to end up on the wrong end of a gun, I was asked to help. I make no apologies for my actions. I did my duty. The investigations I was involved in were successful, which is why I have been maligned and despised throughout the unit. So be it."

"Then tell me, Vizier, just how successful are you with missing persons?"

"I haven't solved them all, but I sure have made a dent, Sheriff. Sometimes you never find people. That's just the way it is. I do, however, know what I'm doing and my record reflects that."

"Yeah, I checked on that, too. It does. The problem is, this ain't the city. We are surrounded by swamps out here. It's a whole different thing searching for folks in the swamp."

"Yes, sir, I suppose it is. I have been in the swamp plenty, Sheriff. I grew up out here. I might not be some swamp rat *coonass* with a hound dog nose, but I am resourceful."

"Well, you're gonna have to be. We got a

big problem ever since those storms came through. We have a backlog and not enough manpower or resources to tackle them."

"I look forward to the challenge, Sheriff. Does that mean you'll take me on?"

"Now hold on, I didn't say that. I might consider giving you a run and see how you do, but there are a few things we need to get straight first. Everyone 'round here knows your rep. Not many people are going to be too happy to help you out. On top of that, seems you have a history of abandoning your priorities whenever things suit you."

"Now, just wait a minute, Sheriff."

"Don't interrupt me, Vizier. I wasn't finished. I did my research. I know all about you taking off and leaving your mother to languish out here all alone, college boy. It was my department that made sure she got the proper funeral, one at which you were nowhere to be found. I also know that you happened to be far, far away when Katrina hit. Your home was underwater and your precinct needed you. You were high and dry in the Rocky Mountains. Now, I am sure you have all kinds of reasons and excuses to back you up. I don't want to hear them. Just understand one thing – you better be around when we need you. Got it?"

"Got it, Sheriff."

Nick was livid, but didn't show it. He had

BILLY

a much better poker face than these rednecks; he needed one back in the city. Fuck this backwards hick, he thought. What the hell did he know?

"When can I start?"

"Right now. Deputy Arceneuax will show you to your desk. Don't get too comfortable there either, I expect you to work for a living. I've got enough desk jockeys around here as it is."

Nicholas walked to an open area with several desks scattered around. The deputy brought him a box filled with assorted files.

"Good to meet you, Vizier. As you know, I'm Deputy Arceneaux. You can call me Dean. We got a doozie here for you to start on. It should be right up your alley."

The deputy unceremoniously dumped the heavy box on Nick's desk and smiled to himself as he walked away. Nick was sure that he was being set up for failure; it was common to be initiated with a case no one wanted on your first day. It wasn't the first time he encountered some impossible-to-solve cold case, or followed up some mishandled clusterfuck of someone else's making. It's okay, thought Nick. I'll just have to show these backwoods *coonasses* what a college-educated city-boy can do.

CLAYTON E. SPRIGGS

Chapter Eleven

Missing

It didn't take long to understand why Galliano hired him on the spot, or why the sheriff needed Nick to start right away. There had already been a considerable backlog of missing persons files prior to Hurricane Katrina and Hurricane Rita, and now there were ten times the number. The region had been hit hard by the two storms, and resources were stretched thin.

Organization was an even bigger problem. Much of the population had been displaced, moving from here to there and back, which made it almost impossible to find any particular person at any particular location when needed. State records were often missing, many of them destroyed by the widespread flooding throughout the state, and although an influx of volunteers poured in from the rest of the country, sometimes this only made things more convoluted.

The current box on Nick's desk attested to this. The more he read about the timeline of events and people involved in the case, the more Nick shook his head in dismay. Whatever could go wrong evidently did go wrong.

The trouble seemed to start when a family of ignorant *coonasses* refused to evacuate to higher ground prior to Katrina. When they were never heard from again, a rescue party was sent to find them. Naturally, the family lived deep in the swamp where only a few select and unavailable locals could find them. This did nothing to discourage the college-aged out-of-state volunteers from securing a boat and setting out into the wetlands without any idea of what they were getting into. Generation Millennium was the name the group gave itself at the time – proud of its mission and sure of its successful completion.

Nick almost found it amusing thinking about the ill-fated mission. He wondered how long it took them to get lost and how long after that before they realized what a terrible mistake they'd all made. Ah, the confidence and ignorance of youth, thought

BILLY

Nick. He could imagine some of his college buddies doing something just as stupid and how quickly things would have gotten terribly out of hand. The difference was, most of the people he went to college with were from Louisiana and had enough sense to stay out of the swamp.

When the search party never materialized again, a Coast Guard chopper was sent in to look for them. By the third day, the search was called off. Another hurricane was looming on the horizon. Hurricane Rita slammed into the coast on September twenty-fourth, less than a month after Hurricane Katrina made ground. By the time the worst was over and the water had subsided, too much time had passed to hold out much hope for the missing crew. The Coast Guard did their best, but nothing was ever found.

Nick leafed through the folders, each one containing a short bio and photo of the person missing. There was Corey Phillips, a twenty-four year old man from Akron, Ohio, who recently graduated from Syracuse University with a degree in Biology. Probably the leader of the ill-fated mission, thought Nick, who imagined the boy mistakenly thought his classroom time and fresh diploma gave him some kind of expertise in the foreboding environment of the Atchafalaya Wetlands. Jeremy Wilson was a twenty-year-old Junior at Brigham Young University, a bright young man with a bright future who had lived his entire life in the deserts of Utah and had no business whatsoever trampling through the swamps in the Deep South during hurricane season. Margaret Evans was even younger, a nineteen-year-old girl from Iowa, who delayed her first year of college to volunteer with her church group to help the survivors of the devastated region recover as best they could. Ashley Gilmore rounded out the group. Ashley, a twenty-two-year-old pre-pharmacy student from Franklin, Tennessee, had expressed an interest in attending Xavier University in New Orleans and readily volunteered her time and energy in the area's recovery with the realization that it might be her future home while she worked on her graduate degree.

Nick felt sorry for the missing volunteers and their families. Each of them had a bright future to look forward to, and each of them had made a valiant effort in giving their time in order to help others. It was sad that, in the end, they gave their young lives in the process. Nick knew that, by this time, the chances of any of them surviving in the hostile environment was pretty slim, as were his chances of finding out their fates. He

BILLY

shook his head as he rifled through the rest of the files in front of him. If it weren't for those damn Cajuns refusing to evacuate, none of this would have ever happened, he thought. Finally, Nick found what he was looking for. He quickly determined that the source of all of the problems and the place where he would begin his investigation was one and the same.

"The St. Pierres," Nick said aloud to himself. He was determined that he would get to know them well.

CLAYTON E. SPRIGGS

Chapter Twelve

Dit Mon La Verite'

Nicholas started his investigation from his desk. He asked his fellow deputies what they knew about the missing youths and the St. Pierre family. Turns out, they didn't know much. They all knew what everyone else knew about the missing kids, namely, that they went out into the swamp in a rented boat without a guide and a clue as to what they were doing and promptly got lost. Hurricane Rita came right on their heels and eliminated any chance of survival that they might have had. As yet, no trace of the group had been found. Nick was hired to find them, and as Sheriff Galliano put it, "he wasn't going to find them sitting at his desk."

The St. Pierre clan was tenuously known

around the sheriff's office. They lived deep in the swamp at some place called *Bayou Noir*, which, as it turned out, only a select few people knew how to get to. Occasionally, one or the other would surface in town to attend Sunday Service over at St. Gabriel's and pick up a few items at the local store. Deputy Arceneaux seemed to know the most about them, which wasn't much, but he readily shared the information he had with Nick one day over a tray of boiled crawfish.

"They pretty much kept to themselves," Dean said. "The only real neighbors they had were the Landrys, and I'm not sure where they are right now. Last I heard, most of them were over in Lake Charles, but I'd bet they'll be back soon. Their family's been here a long time, and I doubt a couple of storms gonna keep them out for long."

"Yeah, that's what I heard, too," Nick replied as he sucked on another of the delicious critters in front of him. "I'm still hoping that one of the Landrys will show up soon to help out with the search, but I'm not going to wait on it. The sheriff gave me a few names of a couple of locals that might help out, but I haven't had much luck on that front yet. I figure I still have a little ground work to do before I go riding out into the swamp. I am not about to make the same mistake those kids did."

BILLY

Dean nodded at the sentiment. "Yep, that's the smart thing to do. Jean Landry might show up soon, but I'm not sure how much help he'll be. He was the closest thing to a friend the St. Pierres had, but even he didn't like to go out there if he didn't have to. The St. Pierres were a strange bunch, from what I've heard. Not too bright and not too friendly is the best way I can put it."

"Tell me more about them, if you can," Nick said. "How many are there?"

"Five, that I know of," answered Dean. "There's Poppie – he's the patriarch of the family and one of the meanest sons of bitches you're ever going to meet. Then there's Dorcelia, his wife – a saintly woman who puts up with that man for who knows what reason. Besides that, there's two boys, T-Roy and Justin, and Lillian, the girl. Lillian's a pretty young thing, too, but quiet as a mouse. Rumor has it she ran off with some feller from out of town, and I can't say as I blame her. Either way, she hasn't been seen around here for quite some time."

"You think there's any chance they survived out there?" Nick asked.

"I doubt it," answered Dean. "Water got pretty high from what I heard. Of course, ain't no one been able to get out there and check on them, so there's no way to know for sure."

"How about those Coast Guard helicopters? Why haven't they been able to find anything?"

"Well, you have to understand what it's like out there. Their house is probably little more than a shack built on sticks. It's been there for ages and probably overgrown with vines and weeds. You would almost have to know where it is ahead of time and be right on top of it to see it, and even that's not a given. Besides, with all of those stupid stories going around, no one's going out there unless they have to."

"Stories?" Nick asked. "What stories?"

Dean paused for a moment before taking another swig of his beer. The crawfish were spicy, and it was all he could do to keep his acid reflux at bay.

"You know these Cajuns, Nick. A lot of them have lived out here their whole lives with little education and even less interaction with the outside world. The St. Pierres might be the worst of them, but they ain't the only ones. Anyway, I have heard stories about ghosts and spirits and supernatural creatures haunting the swamp since I was a child. Most of them are just that – ghost stories no one takes seriously, told just to scare the little ones."

"Yeah, I've heard a few of those myself," Nick recollected.

BILLY

"Well, lately, some of the stories have been getting scary. There's talk of some kind of swamp monster roaming around and killing things. It's got some of the locals spooked, even some of the ones you'd think would know better." Dean shook his head while telling the story, "Ignorant *coonasses*," he laughed. "Fucking swamp monster."

"Yeah, it does sound kinda stupid," Nick agreed. "Maybe it's a distant relative of Bigfoot?"

The men laughed.

Dean thought about the incident on Bayou Blue Road and the missing Louisiana Gas employee. No trace of the man had ever been found, despite the exhaustive search they had conducted. By the copious amount of blood left at the site, there was little doubt the man met a gruesome fate as the meal of a hungry predator. It was assumed that the guilty party had been an alligator of gigantic proportions, although whispers of another unknown beast made their way around.

Dean remembered the sensation of being watched when he came upon the scene, and it made him shudder. He never saw whatever it was that had given him that feeling, but lately his slumber was haunted by visions of a demonic spirit gazing upon him from the darkness of the swamp. He promptly dismissed his misgivings, realizing how childish they were and changed the subject.

"You're alright, Nick," Dean said. "I guess you know there's talk going on about you behind your back."

Nick nodded, but kept quiet.

"Typical shit about your stint in Internal Affairs and all. I want you to know none of that shit means nothin' to me. From what I've heard about Orleans Parish, someone had to take a stand. The way I figure it, if you've got nothin' to hide, there's nothin' to worry about."

"Everyone's got something to hide, Dean. I don't care about any of that now, anyway. I'm not here for that. I'm here to help out in whatever way I can. Right now, I'm here to find those kids and anyone else that might be missing. I just hope I don't run into that monster in the process."

The two men laughed again.

"Yeah, it does sound kind of stupid," Dean said, shaking his head. "Those rumors have been going around for awhile now, but ever since the storms hit, everyone seems to get in on it. I don't know if it's because everything is so uncertain now or because of some kind of post traumatic stress, but people are swearing they've seen or heard all of these ridiculous things. I put most of the blame on that girl they found."

BILLY

Nick almost choked on the crawfish tail in his mouth.

"Girl?" he asked. "What girl?"

"I know what you're thinking, but don't read too much into it, Nick," Dean tried to explain. "There's some girl that was found a couple of months ago that was lost in the swamp. No one really knows who she is, but she ain't exactly the best historian. They got her locked up in the mental ward over at St. Elizabeth's. She claims that there is some monster that lives in an old plantation in the swamp and hunts and kills people for sport. Fuel to the fire is all I can say. Never mind we live in the twenty-first century and never mind how many times I've tried to tell people there are no such things as swamp monsters or whatever. Instead, these dumbass inbred hicks believe some outlandish story told by some nut in the loony bin. Go figure."

Dean gulped down the last of his beer and headed for the bathroom leaving Nick alone at the table. What the hell has he gotten himself into? Ghosts, unknown creatures, plantations in the swamp inhabited by monsters, insane ramblings by an unknown lunatic in the local asylum; one theory more ridiculous than the next and at the heart of his budding investigation, the situation almost made Nick choke. He contemplated how likely it was that he was being set up in some elaborate prank. Either way, he concluded that he would be visiting a special guest of St. Elizabeth's Mental Health Unit before long. If the joke was on him, he only hoped that, at the end, they would all be laughing. Deep inside something told him that there was going to be nothing funny about it.

Chapter Thirteen

St. Elizabeth's

The best word Nicholas could use to describe the facilities at St. Elizabeth's Institute for the Mentally Ill was 'creepy'. Although it was built in the nineteen twenties, the Victorian architecture gave it a haunted house feel. Nick thought that, even when it was newly constructed, the building probably looked old. He was no expert in mental health, but Nick questioned the wisdom of housing paranoid schizophrenics in such a setting.

The interior of the building is not any better than the exterior, thought Nick. Even with the occasional modern upgrades, there was no undoing the eeriness that the architecture provided. The attempt at sterilizing the environment only made it more impersonal and unwelcoming. Every pore in Nick's body told him to get out of there as soon as he was able. He could only imagine the terror of being locked inside such a place against your will, even for the sane. For those who suffer the unimaginable horrors of mental illness, it must have been unbearable.

After an extended wait and a round of credential checking, Nick was escorted by a pair of rather large gentlemen wearing nondescript white scrubs into a back office. He couldn't help but notice how different the décor was once he arrived in the back. The walls were painted in warm, pastel colors that blended nicely with the Berber carpet and solid wood furniture. There were pictures of smiling family members on every wall, along with proud displays of diplomas and awards that attested to the unquestionable qualifications of the people in charge.

Nick waited in an outer office while being completely ignored by a middle-aged secretary with large horn-rimmed glasses and an absurd amount of makeup on her face. He tried not to stare at the painted-on eyebrows that were uneven and sitting higher on the woman's face than the place where she had shaved off her actual eyebrows. He couldn't understand the

BILLY

rationale of such an act of facial vandalism, but he never had the guts to ask why anyone would do that to themselves.

After another extended wait, Nicholas was called into the inner sanctum of one Dr. Theodore Newsome. Dr. Newsome was the Chief Psychiatrist at St. Elizabeth's — not surprising considering his pedigree, history of attending Ivy League institutions, and the plethora of letters behind his name. His appearance was anything but imposing. Standing only five foot four and as thin as a rail, the good doctor looked like he might even tumble-over from the weight of his spectacles. The Orville Redenbacher bow tie and leather elbow patches on the man's sport coat eliminated any amount of smoothness the slight man might have possessed, and Nick couldn't help but wonder if he smoked a pipe like the patriarch on My Three Sons. Dr. Theodore Newsome was exactly what Nick was expecting the chief headshrinker was going to be.

"I understand you're here to see one of our patients, Officer Vizier?" the doctor asked.

"Detective. Detective Vizier," corrected Nick. He didn't care how many letters or awards the doctor had, he wasn't the least impressed or intimidated. "Yes, Doctor, I am."

"You are aware that some of your

colleagues have interrogated the poor girl on several occasions already."

"Yes, I'm aware. Unfortunately, they didn't do a very good job of it."

"No, they didn't. To be perfectly frank with you, Detective, they made a mess of it."

"Which is why I'm here," said Nick.

"Which is why you're here," stated the doctor, waving his arms to signify the office around them. "You need to understand a few things, Detective. The patient is in a very fragile state, and although we've been making progress, it's been slow. There are still so many things that she's been unable to tell us, and we have a long road ahead of us. Even the slightest amount of stress or undue pressure and we're all back to square one. Now, I know that your office is trying to do everything you can to help out, and I respect the work you do. You just have to respect what it is that we do. In the end, the girl's health is my primary concern and everything else is secondary to that. I'm sure you understand."

"So, what are you saying then, Doctor? Are you denying me access to the girl?"

"The girl, as you call her, is my patient. My only concern is for her. She has a name; a name that even she won't tell us at this time. She has lived through something that has traumatized her beyond her ability to cope.

BILLY

In response, her mind has closed off much of her memory in an attempt to protect herself. In order to treat her, we are faced with allowing her the comfort of putting the past behind her while at the same time trying to help her face her fears in order to regain who she once was. It is a difficult task, maybe an impossible one, and we can't have our progress damaged by your efforts, however important you feel they may be."

"With all due respect, Doctor, you have your job to do and I have mine. The girl is a witness, whether she knows what she saw or not, and I am well within my jurisdiction to question her as I see fit. I appreciate your concerns, and I will go about my duties with the utmost care, but I intend to question the witness all the same."

"With all due respect, Detective, the girl as you call her, is under my care. I can and will grant you access to her as I see fit. If you think you can override that, think again. You may use my phone to call the sheriff or anyone else you want, and I assure you, they will tell you the same thing."

"You don't know her name any more than I do, Doctor, so why is it that you assume that my referring to her as the girl is demeaning in some way?"

"We call her Jane, a name we give to all female patients when we don't know their proper name. We call her Jane, and I pointed out that she is not just a 'girl' because I want to make sure you understand that she is a person. She is someone's daughter, maybe someone's sister, maybe someone's mother, maybe someone's girlfriend or wife, not just a witness or a girl for you to interrogate to help you in your quest, however noble it may be."

"I understand your point, Doctor, and it is well taken. Please, let me assure you of not only my intentions, but of my qualifications. It's true that I'm not a psychiatrist or psychologist and have no advance degrees in mental health, but I'm not just some local deputy out to stir the pot. I'm aware of the girl's – of Jane's – situation, and I'm grateful to you that we are even having this talk. Your concerns are valid, but then again, so are mine. Perhaps there is some way we can come to a mutual agreement?"

"I'm listening, Detective."

"We can talk to her together, if you wish. We can go over my questions ahead of time as well. There are only a few things I would like to discuss with the...with Jane, and I realize that we may not get to those. Surely, there is some way that we can make this happen, Doctor."

Dr. Newsome sat quietly for a few moments, contemplating the officer's

BILLY

request. He could see that the man was not going to go away quietly, and eventually he would call the doctor's bluff. It was true that the doctor had some say so over what the police could or couldn't do, but it was also true that if push came to shove, the police were going to have their way. Things would be much better if the attorneys were kept out of it, a sentiment that would be equally shared by Nick.

"Well, perhaps there is a way this can work, Detective. There's a big problem that you may not be aware of, however."

"And what's that?"

"The girl, Jane, is almost comatose the majority of the time. She isn't exactly non-responsive, but it's not like she's going to be answering any questions, either."

"I am not sure I understand you, Doctor. She was questioned in the past and had all kinds of things to say. Maybe most of what she said didn't make sense, but she was talking, alright."

"Yes, that's true. Unfortunately, things have changed somewhat since then. Like I stated earlier, your men made a mess of things. The interrogations resulted in the poor girl's inability to accept the memories they produced, which, in turn, led her to the state that she is currently in. Follow me, Detective, and see for yourself."

The men left the doctor's office and made their way down a labyrinth of identical hallways and locked doors until they came upon an open room with a dozen or so people roaming around. The exterior walls were lined with big windows covered with iron grates that overlooked the well-manicured lawn of the medical facility. Most of the people, who Nick assumed were patients, sat alone, fidgeting with their fingers or rocking back and forth in a state of sedated stupor. A few wandered about, talking to themselves in hushed voices while eyeing those around them suspiciously. In a rocking chair facing one of the windows, sat a girl with long brown hair and a pale complexion, her face expressionless and her eyes blank, seemingly unaware of everything around her. Nick knew in an instant that this was Jane.

The detective and the doctor approached slowly until Nick saw the girl's face up close for the first time. He tensed at the sight, a reaction that was not lost on the psychiatrist. The two men quietly walked out of the room and down one of the long hallways before the doctor spoke first.

"Are you going to tell me, or do I have to ask?"

"Her name's not Jane – it's Margaret."

Chapter Fourteen

Margaret

"I appreciate you coming out here, Detective, and now that we know who Jane – I mean Margaret – is, we might be able to better help her," Dr. Newsome said. "But even so, going too aggressively down the path you are suggesting could cause irreparable damage to the patient."

"I understand your concerns, Doctor, but I don't see how we have any other options," Nick explained. "There are three other kids out there, and we have to do everything we can to try to find them. She's the only one who knows what happened, and we need to find out as much as we can from her for those other kids to have any chance at all."

"With all due respect, how much chance do

you think they have as it is? Jane – I mean Margaret – has been here three months already. There's almost no chance of survival for the others. Besides, once her family's been notified, I am sure she'll be moved closer to them, and you and your fellow officers will have to run everything through their people."

"True, Doctor, which is all the more reason we do this now. The longer we wait, the less chance we have of finding those kids, alive or dead. And you're right, Margaret does have a family and we'll have to respect their wishes. I might remind you that those other three kids have families, too. We have a duty to them to do everything we can for their kids."

Dr. Newsome said nothing, but he knew the detective was right. Sure, he could stall the man long enough until the girl was moved and he could wash his hands of the entire mess, but deep down he knew this wasn't an option. He wanted to know what really happened out there as much as the policeman did. The doctor knew that, as risky as it was, having the girl face the truth was the only way she would ever be able to heal.

"You've seen the reports, Detective," Dr. Newsome said. "The tale she told about her experience in the swamp sounded more like a nightmare than anything plausible. Worse

BILLY

yet, ever since word got out about her wild story, the superstitious locals have been running scared. This, I blame on your people. No one from this facility would have spread such private and disturbing recollections of a mental patient. How do I know this won't happen again?"

"You have legitimate concerns, Doctor," Nick replied.

He knew only too well that the doctor was probably right about the rumors being spread by people in his own department. His ill-advised stint with the Internal Affairs Division taught him how untrustworthy some of his fellow officers were. "Still, I don't see any other course of action. Surely, there is some way we can move forward on this by working together."

"Well, there might be one way," Dr. Newsome replied.

"I'm all ears," Nick answered.

"I've been studying the patient's unique situation closely since her arrival here and have been considering a more aggressive approach than the one we've taken. I was going to wait a little while longer to see if Jane – Margaret – would start to come along on her own. Of course, since she'll most likely be transferred to another facility out-of-state soon, she'll likely regress. A change in her surroundings and care by unfamiliar personnel will undoubtedly be traumatic for her, and she'll need yet another period of adjustment to compensate. Whatever chance we have for a breakthrough at this time will be lost."

"Then, by all means, now is the time."

"It just very well may be."

"What did you have in mind, Doctor?"

"Hypnotherapy."

"Hypnosis? Is that real?"

"It's very real, Detective, and it just might work."

The more the psychiatrist explained the procedure to Nick, the more he thought it was their best chance. As it was, the girl's fragile state made it all but impossible to question her and expect to get anything useful in return. Putting the girl in a trance might enable them to probe the memories that she worked so hard to forget. As long as they proceeded with caution, they may even pull it off without the poor girl consciously reliving the terror that caused her so much pain. It wasn't going to be easy, since both of the men were required to be present and interrogate the girl. The entire endeavor would require a great deal of preparation, finesse, and luck. Unfortunately for them, they had little time to prepare, but they agreed that it was in everyone's best interest to move forward with the plan.

BILLY

The two men discussed the procedure and what they wanted to accomplish. They knew they had one shot at it and were determined to get the most out of it that they could. It was agreed that they'd meet again the next morning before breakfast to map out their roles, then commence with the hypnosis at ten o'clock. As Nick was walking out, Dr. Newsome handed him an envelope.

"This is Margaret's file," he said. "Read through it tonight and bring it back with you tomorrow morning. I trust I don't need to tell you that it's confidential."

"I understand, Doctor," Nick replied. "I'll see you in the morning."

When Nick got home that night, he sat at his small kitchen table and looked through the contents of the file. There wasn't much in it. A list of medications and treatments, all standard stuff as far as Nick could see, as well as a few notes by the various staff at St. Elizabeth's that were, at best, vague and nondescript. Most of the details of the girl's discovery and subsequent transfer to the hospital, the detective already knew.

He put the papers down and sighed. What a mess. If only the girl could answer a dozen questions or so without all of the drama they could just move on, he thought. Nick knew that he'd have to be patient with the girl, and he tried to be sympathetic, though he lacked the full comprehension of the girl's incapacity. Mental illness was one thing he didn't fully understand or appreciate, even with his vast experience dealing with the depraved and sick individuals that came with a career in law enforcement. He remembered how the girl sat in her chair staring blankly at the world around her. He knew what he was up against.

Nick started to put the contents of the file back into the envelope when he noticed a few pages of typewritten notes that he'd previously missed. Upon closer inspection, he saw that they were transcripts of a session that Dr. Newsome had held with Margaret when she was first admitted under his care. He read through them with astonishment. He could clearly see that, at that time, the girl was not only responsive, she was full of details about her experience in the swamp. Her timeline was a complete jumble as she went back and forth without any discernible logical fashion. Then the whole thing ended abruptly, with the girl going into hysterics. Oh, this was going to be fun, thought the detective.

From what he could determine, the group got lost almost right away when they headed into the Atchafalaya Basin. They rode around in a futile effort to find their way only to eventually come across a house

BILLY

hidden way out in the swamp. A quick search had been made, and no survivors were found. After that, the story took a wild turn. Random details of bad weather, being lost, snakes and alligators, and infighting amongst the crew. All of this deteriorated in tales of a decrepit antebellum plantation inhabited by a swamp monster and days of trampling around in the wetlands without food or water.

"Fucking swamp monster?" Nick laughed to himself. There was little doubt that the girl had been terrified at being lost all alone in the swamp, surrounded by cold-blooded hungry reptiles with which she was completely unfamiliar. It was only natural that her brain would misinterpret her surroundings in the dire situation that she was in.

Nick started to understand the magnitude of what the psychiatrist dealt with every day. He began to understand the very real existence of the unreal when faced with the unexplainable. When trapped in the desert without water, some people see mirages; when afraid in the dark, some people see ghosts; when alone in the woods, some people see Bigfoot, unexplained lights in the sky and some people see flying saucers. Lost in the swamp, Margaret saw a monster.

CLAYTON E. SPRIGGS

Chapter Fifteen

Trance

Nickolas arrived promptly at six a.m. at St. Elizabeth's and was escorted to Dr. Newsome's office without delay. He waited another forty-five minutes for the doctor to arrive. Nick was not amused.

"Sorry I'm late, Detective," Dr. Newsome said dismissively. "I hope you brought Margaret's file with you."

Nick could see that the doctor was used to being in charge. No explanation as to why he was tardy was offered, and no concern for the waste of the detective's time was apparent. Nick was sure that if the tables had been turned, the good doctor would be beside himself with indignation. *I bet he's a real gem to work with for all of the nurses and* other healthcare professionals, thought the detective. Of course, Nick knew he was depending on the doctor so he could move forward with the investigation, and he had no choice but to put up with the man's inconsideration. Deep down, the detective figured the doctor also knew this and was enjoying every minute of it. Fucking passive-aggressive son-of-a-bitch, thought Nick.

"Yes, I did," answered Nick. "Pretty interesting reading, particularly the part about the swamp monster that lives on a plantation in the swamp."

Dr. Newsome looked at the detective to see if he could detect a smirk, but the man was poker faced. Good, the doctor thought; no need for sarcasm at the expense of the poor, distraught young lady.

"We should go over a few things about the procedure as well as lay down a few ground rules before we begin," the doctor stated.

"Absolutely, Doctor," Nick said. "You're the expert here. I'll be happy to follow along and help in any way I can."

"Good, I am glad to hear that. Here is a list of questions that I would like to address if we get the opportunity," Dr. Newsome said as he handed a pad with some barely-legible writing on it. "Feel free to add a few of your own, as long as I approve of them first, and we'll see what we get to when the procedure

BILLY

commences. I'm not sure how successful we'll be, nor how long we'll be able to maintain the questions before things go south."

"Of course, Dr. Newsome. I've jotted down a few questions of my own, although I see that you've already included a number of them," Nick said while glancing over the list. "I can't help but notice that a good portion of your questions have to do with Margaret's overall therapy and not so much with the investigation of the missing search party. While I appreciate your attempt at using this opportunity to provide as much therapy as possible for the poor girl, I do want to remind you of why we're here."

"Of why *we're* here, or of why *you're* here, Detective?"

"I'm not going to play games with you, Doctor. You know what I'm getting at. If we only have a short window of opportunity, we need, *I* need, to get to the heart of the matter. I thought we'd agreed on that issue."

Dr. Newsome stared at the detective for a moment before relenting. "Of course, Detective. You may have a point. We can get to the heart of the matter, as you put it, and see where it leads us."

The men looked over the list of questions, scratching out a few of them and numbering the rest. The overall strategy was to prompt Margaret into recalling her experiences in the swamp and, in particular, the fates and whereabouts of the missing crew. They would attempt to guide her in a logical, chronological order to help Nick in his own search for the three. Once the list of questions was compiled and edited, Dr. Newsome accompanied Nick down to one of the unoccupied rooms where the therapy would take place.

The room was moderately comfortable, actually very comfortable compared to the rest of the facility. The floor was covered with a medium gray carpet and the walls were painted a light brown color. Soft, indirect lighting made the room almost too dark, but relaxing. The only sound heard was the faint rustling of the air blowing out of the vent overhead. A comfortable, softly-cushioned chair sat in the center of the room facing two wooden chairs and a one-way mirror that hid a tripod and video camera. Doctor Newsome gave some last-minute instructions to his assistants and re-emphasized the importance of keeping things calm and low-key during the interview.

"The last time we addressed what happened out there, poor Margaret became hysterical," Dr. Newsome explained. "After that, she withdrew into an almost catatonic state. Let's try not to let that happen again, Detective."

BILLY

Nick nodded and waited for the arrival of their guest.

Margaret appeared at the doorway, escorted by one of the nurses and trailed by two orderlies, just in case. The girl barely displayed any knowledge of where she was or who was around her. She sat in the chair provided and stared straight ahead without making a sound. Dr. Newsome sat in the chair directly in front of the girl, and Nick sat in the chair at his side. Between them, perched on a small, round table sat an object that Nick guessed had something to do with the procedure. The doctor glanced toward the mirror on the wall, and then nodded to the nurse, who nodded back before leaving the room. Nick knew that the girl had been injected with a mild sedative prior to her arrival and figured that the nurse's nod confirmed this to the doctor.

The lights dimmed even further, apparently controlled by the assistants in the other room, and Dr. Newsome reached over and carefully flicked a switch on the back of the object that sat on the table in the middle of the dark room. A strange, rotating strobe light flickered on and off in quick succession, accompanied by the light clicking sound of a metronome. A center disk spiraled in a counter-clockwise motion, drawing one's gaze into a center that had no end. The apparatus oddly reminded Nick of the satellite images he watched on the news months before — those unforgettable pictures of a vast, swirling cloud of destruction descending on his state, his city, his home. He choked back the tears that suddenly welled up in his eyes, thinking how weirdly appropriate it was for the ghost of Katrina to draw the broken girl closer to her darkest fears. Moments later, the doctor began.

"Margaret, do you hear me?"

The girl blinked at the sound of her name, spoken to her for the first time in months. Her lips pursed as if she were about to say something, but she withdrew again into the nether reaches of her mind.

"Margaret, I want you to listen to me. I want you to focus on the shiny object in front of you."

For a few moments, there was no reaction from the girl. Nick's heart began to sink as the girl showed no sign of understanding. Then, Margaret's eyes moved to the object in front of her. Her gaze fixated on the flashing light, her head almost imperceptibly nodding in time to the clicking noise.

"Good," Dr. Newsome continued. "Watch the flashing light closely. You can feel it as it draws you in. You see nothing else, feel nothing else, see only the light, hear only my voice."

BILLY

Silence enveloped the room. Margaret's eyes stared intently at the circle of light until they began to close.

"Now, you are getting sleepy. Your eyelids are growing heavy. It's okay, allow them to close. You see the light in your mind. You are sleeping, but still awake. You see the flashing light; you hear my voice. You are asleep, but still awake. You see the flashing light; you hear my voice. You are asleep."

A moment of silence passed, only the sounds of the clicking metronome and air vent overhead could be heard.

The doctor continued, "What is your name?"

"Margaret," the girl whispered.

"Margaret, you are with your friends. You are in a boat, heading out to rescue the poor people stranded by the storm. Tell me where you are"

"I'm sitting next to Ash, Jerry's up front."

"Who else is there?"

"Corey. He's driving the boat. It's hot outside, but, thank God, there's a breeze. The water stinks."

"Where are you going?"

"We're on a small river. I don't know where we're heading, but Corey says he knows."

The doctor paused for a moment, allowing the girl's memory to guide her.

"How long have you been on the river now?"

"The river's gone. We're on some canal. It's hard to tell where we are. It all looks the same. Jerry says we're lost. I think Ash is scared; she's squeezing my hand. It's sticky. There's bugs everywhere."

Dr. Newsome paused again before taking a deep breath and continuing the questioning with a soothing, comforting tone.

"Time has passed. Where are you now?"

"I don't know. We're lost. Jerry and Corey started to argue and then Ashley began screaming. Now, everyone is quiet. We're going somewhere, I don't know where."

The doctor glanced toward Nick, who shook his head in dismay. The two thought the same thing. What had possessed the youngsters to go out into the swamp without a guide in the first place?

"Did you find something?"

"There's a house, a house on sticks. It's quiet. It was loud awhile ago; now it's quiet. I'm scared. I want to go home."

"Did you go into the house?"

"Jerry and Corey did; they had to. It's why we came."

"Is there anyone in the house?"

"Jerry went in with Corey to look. Jerry's painting something on the wall out front. He looks pale. Corey's coming out now. He's

BILLY

talking with Jerry. They're coming back to the boat."

"Go on."

"Corey said there were no survivors. He said there were people inside, but they must've drowned. Jerry said it was hard to tell; the animals must've gotten to them. Ashley asked if anyone went into the attic."

"Did they?"

"Corey says no. Jerry said he couldn't understand it. They would've lived if they'd gone up there, but they didn't go. He asked Corey what was up there. Corey said there was nothing up there. He's not talking much about it, which is weird. Corey likes to talk. Ash says something's wrong. Why didn't they go into the attic?"

The doctor looked over at the detective with a questionable look on his face. Nick looked back and shrugged. Why didn't they go into the attic? Ashley had been right; something was definitely wrong.

"Where are you going next?"

"It's starting to drizzle. We need to get out of the rain, but no one wants to go inside the house. It's creepy. We're trying to find some shelter. We're lost. I'm scared."

"It's okay, Margaret. Where are you going now?"

"We're lost. Jerry is arguing with Corey. He says that we're just going further into the swamp. The rain is getting heavier, the water is getting rough. Ash is crying."

"Did you find somewhere to get out of the rain?"

"We had to. I didn't want to get out of the boat, but the water's getting rough. It's windy, and the rain is coming down hard now. There's an island. There's some rocks we can tie the boat to. The island is overgrown with cypress and oak trees. They're covered with moss. We find a dry spot underneath some tall trees. Oh my God!"

"What is it? What do you see?"

"They're not trees. Not all of them are trees. They're pillars. There's an old staircase, an old fireplace. We're at an old plantation. It's starting to get dark. I'm scared."

"Shhhh, it's okay Margaret, it's okay. What are y'all doing now?"

"Corey went to get some firewood. He didn't come back. Where is he? Why didn't he come back? Jerry wants to go look for him, but Ash is getting hysterical. Where's Corey? It's starting to thunder. I want to go home."

"Did Corey return?"

"No. Jerry said he'd go look real quick and he'd be right back. He just left. Oh no!"

"What's happening now?"

"Oh no, oh no," Margaret began to cry.

BILLY

Dr. Newsome paused for a moment, not sure if they should proceed or stop right there. He glanced over toward Nick, who was staring intently at the girl, hanging on to every word.

"Did Jerry come back?" Nick asked.

"No. He screamed; I know I heard it. I told Ash it was just the thunder, but I know it was Jerry. He's not coming back, he's not coming back."

"So now, it's just you and Ashley?" Nick continued, much to the doctor's displeasure. He could see things were starting to spin out of control, but he knew the detective wasn't going to stop now.

"Yes, I mean, no. No, there's someone else, something else there. I'm scared. Ash is crying. I can't get her to stop. She has to stop. The thing will hear us."

"What thing?" asked Nick.

"It's coming. Shut up, Ash, its coming. I see it. It's standing in the rain, when the lightning flashes, I can see it. It's looking right at us. Oh my God! It sees us. It has red eyes; red eyes staring right at us. Shut up, Ash, shut up for God's sake!"

"What's happening now?" Nick asked.

"I don't see it. It's gone. No, it's not. I know it's here. Oh my God! It's here! Ash screamed at it. She told it to go away. She told the monster to go away. I think it's mad.

It screamed back at us. A loud roar. Ash's running away. No! Oh no, oh no, oh no! The thing got Ash. Oh no!"

The girl broke down, sobbing loudly, tears running down her pale cheeks. Just when Dr. Newsome was going to stop the whole procedure, Margaret composed herself. She began to speak again, her voice barely above a whisper.

"I'm alone. I don't want to die. I have to get to the boat."

"Where are you?" the doctor asked.

"I'm trying to find the boat. I see the rocks. The boat is by the rocks."

"Are you by the rocks?" Nick asked.

"I hear it. It's coming. I'm hiding behind one of the rocks. The ground is loose; I'm sinking in the mud. I'm too scared to look over the rock. Oh my God! There's a name on the rock. It's a tombstone; I'm lying on a grave. I don't want to die! I'm running to the boat. It's gone, the boat's gone. The thing is right behind me. I'm turning around."

"What do you see?" asked the detective.

"It's a monster. Its red eyes are staring at me. It's covered in blood. Oh no, it's Jerry's blood, its Corey's blood, oh Ash. It has claws, big sharp claws. I'm falling to my knees. It's going to kill and eat me. Sharp teeth, flesh hanging off the teeth. I have to throw up, but I'm too scared. I'm crying. I look at its face

BILLY

once again. I can't look away. It's just staring at me. I plead with it, don't kill me, please. Don't kill me. Hail Mary, full of grace, the Lord is with thee."

The girl's voice trailed off, a blank expression returned to her face. Slowly, her mouth began to move. She was trying to say something. The two men craned their necks and listened intently, trying to make out what the girl was saying.

"Margaret, what do you see?" Nick quietly asked.

"It's just staring at me. Oh no, oh no, oh no. It's smiling at me," she whispered. "He's smiling at me!" Margaret shouted. "He's smiling at me! He's smiling at me! He's smiling at me!"

Margaret was hysterical. She jumped out of the chair and flung herself at the wall before being caught by Dr. Newsome. Two orderlies came abruptly into the room and helped the distraught woman back into the chair, where she collapsed in tears.

"What are you doing now?" asked Nick before the doctor could stop him.

"Running; I'm running. I have to get out of here. I have to get out of here," Margaret sobbed. "I have to get out of here," she cried once more, her voice barely a whisper.

"When I snap my fingers, you will awaken. You will remember nothing. Everything will be as it was. Do you understand me, Margaret?" Dr. Newsome said.

Margaret was no longer listening. She reverted back to her catatonic state. Dr. Newsome kept trying in vain to awaken her from her trance to no avail.

Nick showed himself out, quite certain that he was no longer a welcome guest at St. Elizabeth's. It was true the doctor had warned him about opening up doors that could never be closed. No matter, thought Nick. He had to do what he had to do.

Within days, the girl's family swooped in and had her transferred back to Iowa just as the doctor predicted. The competent staff of the Des Moines Institute of Mental Health worked with their new patient for years. Unfortunately, just like the doctor before them, they were unable to help the girl awaken from her terrible nightmare and the frightening image of the smiling monster that she was forever trying to run away from.

In the end, Nick didn't get much he could use from the hysterical woman. He knew better than to believe in ghosts and monsters. He shared no illusions that he would discover the ruins of a haunted plantation buried deep in the swamp. No, the only thing he found useful was what he determined to be the true source of the girl's

BILLY

nightmares. He knew that's where he was going to start his search – the empty house built on sticks that became a family's tomb. Nick knew the name of that family all too well, the St. Pierres. He knew where he would find them, a place hidden deep amid the cypress trees – a place called *Bayou Noir*.

CLAYTON E. SPRIGGS

Chapter Sixteen

Boo Marie

When Nicholas got back to his desk, he was called into the sheriff's office immediately.

"The good doctor called me up as soon as you left," the sheriff stated. "He went on pissing and moaning about you disturbing the mentally ill. I would've told him to go fuck himself, but I figured you'd done enough damage for one day. Before you even start, let me tell you, I don't give a shit about whatever went down over there, as long as you get results. Tell me. Was it worth your while?"

"Yes, sir, I believe so," Nick replied.

"Personally, I don't know what kind of useful information you're gonna get from some nut locked up in the loony-bin, but you're the one who claims to be the expert, and it's your ass on the line."

"Yeah, I get your point, Sheriff. Unfortunately, the girl locked up over there is the only known survivor of that lost search party. As muddled as her memory is, it's the only thing we have to go on."

"Like I said, Detective, as long as you get results, I don't give a shit how you get them. Of course, there is one thing you might want to keep in mind."

"What's that?" Nick asked.

"Everyone 'round here has heard those stories about that thing hunting people deep in the swamp. You know and I know that's all a bunch of superstitious nonsense, but some of these yokels 'round here believe that shit. You're gonna have to put a search party together to go out there, and you might find those stories could make that difficult to do."

"Yeah, I thought about that, too. Got any suggestions, Sheriff?"

"Jean Landry and his clan are the closest thing you'll find to knowing anything about the St. Pierres. He knows where they live and how to get there. I doubt that he'd be willing to even talk to you though, much less take you out there. If I were you, I'd ask Charlie and Dean to hook you up. They'll know who's who and what's what. Invite them out for a beer or two, and I'm sure

BILLY

they'll help you out."

"Thanks, Sheriff, I appreciate the advice."

"No problem, just get it done before anyone else comes up missing. We need to nip this swamp monster crap in the bud before things get out of hand."

Nicholas could not have agreed with the sheriff more. The ridiculous stories of supernatural creatures lurking in the swamp were only going to make an already difficult job even harder. The sooner they laid these rumors to rest, the better for everyone.

Nick took his boss's advice and asked the two deputies out for drinks that evening. They both readily agreed — so readily that Nick figured the sheriff had already advised them to help out the new guy. Nicholas was thankful for the man's intervention. He was the odd man out and, left to his own devices, he might have a hard time finding locals willing to give him some help — help he desperately needed.

Although Nick had grown up in the area, he was now a city boy at heart. He hated the swamp. He didn't own a boat. He didn't go fishing or hunting and had no idea what he was doing when it came to navigating the vast wetlands he was being forced to enter. Without a local guide, he was dead in the water. Under the circumstances, that was not an expression that gave him any comfort.

CLAYTON E. SPRIGGS

That evening, he met the two men at a local watering hole – Pete's Landing. The place was a little run down, not much bigger than a double-wide trailer, covered with neon signs and with a shell-covered parking lot off of the main highway. There wasn't much competition for clientele, so Pete's generally had a fairly decent size crowd. That Thursday night was no exception.

"Good to see you again, Nick," Dean said as they shook hands. "You remember Deputy Charlie Doucet."

"Yes, sir, I believe so," Nick replied.

"Follow me. We have a table in the back where we can talk," Dean said as he walked toward a corner booth.

"I'm sure the waitress will be over in a few. The service is usually pretty good here," Charlie stated as he and Dean took swigs of their beers. "I hope you don't mind that we started without you."

"Of course not," Nick replied. "I'll just have to play a little catch-up. That is, if y'all don't mind."

"Nope, not a bit," Dean answered.

"Bobby said you're gonna need some help putting a search party together," Charlie stated.

"Yep, sure am."

"Normally that wouldn't be much of a problem. Unfortunately, things haven't been

BILLY

too normal around here lately," Charlie said.

"Everyone's spooked," Dean added. "They're all afraid of that damn thing out there. Damndest thing, if you ask me; a bunch of grown men acting like children, hiding from monsters in their closets."

"It's real enough to them, I suppose," Charlie said. "The stories are coming every day now. People seeing things, hearing things; some of them stories sound pretty spooky, too. You sure you want to go out there?"

"Yeah, well I don't believe in ghosts, or monsters," Nick answered. "I am no fan of the swamp, but if I can go into the projects in New Orleans in the middle of the night looking for gang-banging crack dealers, I sure ain't afraid of some made-up bullshit about the boogey man."

The men laughed.

"No," Dean said. "I guess you aren't. We're in luck; here comes our waitress."

"Hello, Nick. It's been a long time."

Nick looked up and his heart skipped a beat. He felt a lump in his throat, but he pushed through it and feebly responded, "Marie, it's good to see you."

"You two know each other?" Dean asked.

"Obviously, they know each other," Charlie said. "Great detective work there, Deputy."

"I'm sorry to hear about your mother," Marie said. "We're all *en d'oeuille* over her passing."

"Yes," Nick responded. "She was a good woman. It's hard to believe she's gone."

"I saw her from time to time when I went to visit my *parran* at the nursing home. She told me what a success you've become, living over in the city and all. That woman sure loved you."

"Yes, she did. I loved her, too. I'm sorry I didn't come to visit her enough when she was here. Now, all I've got left is regret."

"Enough of that to go around, *Boo*," Marie said before looking up and addressing the others at the table, "Can I get y'all another round?"

"Sure thing," Charlie said. "You can give me and Dean another of the same. What about you, Nick? What're you having?"

"You can bring me one of those, I guess," Nick answered. "On second thought, might want to bring me two; I've got some catching up to do."

After Marie left the table to tend to the drinks, Dean spoke up first. "I didn't know you and Marie knew each other. Small world, I guess."

"Yep, small world," Nick replied. "We dated in high school for a bit. Last I heard, she got married to Ronnie Savoy."

BILLY

"They're divorced," Charlie said. "It's been a couple of years now. Of course, he still comes around and gives her trouble from time to time. His family came into a load of cash from some oil leases, and now the lot of them think they own the parish and everyone in it. Way I hear it, she caught him cattin' around town with a stripper and left him. He's been giving her hell about it ever since."

"I'm sorry to hear that," Nick said. "It's been a long time since I've seen either one of them. I hadn't really thought about them for a long time."

That was a lie. Nick thought about Marie all of the time, even after all these years. Sure, he'd had a number of girlfriends and even a couple of serious relationships in the time since he left and started a life elsewhere, but there was only one first love. Marie LeBlanc was his.

He had to admit to himself that he wasn't entirely unhappy about the failure of her marriage, although he was not pleased that Marie had to suffer any abuse from her ex-husband. Nick remembered Ronald Savoy to be somewhat of a jerk, but he also knew that his opinion of the friend that ran off with the girl he loved wasn't the most objective it could be. Still, he reasoned, even though he had suffered a broken heart in silence for so long over the matter, he felt no joy in seeing Marie struggle because of her unfortunate choice in life.

"Well, here is something that you might be happy to hear about," Dean stated. "We think we have someone that's willing to take you out in search of those lost kids."

"Go on," Nick said.

"Charlie here has a cousin, Frank Guidry, that runs the swamp all of the time and knows it like the back of his hand. Ain't that right, Charlie?"

"Sure does. He and his boy are gator hunters. They go deep into the swamp all the time – day, night, rain, or shine," Charlie answered. "I know for a fact that Bobby's willing to put enough cash on the table for Cap'n Guidry and son to hire a few of their buddies and take you wherever you need to go. Of course, there are a few catches, as always."

"Such as?" asked Nick.

Before Charlie could answer, Marie was back at the table with the drinks. They resumed casual conversation until she left again to tend to the other customers vying for her attention.

"For one thing," Dean answered, "you have to keep the talk about that swamp monster to a minimum. Some of them boys are highly superstitious, and they aren't going to be too

BILLY

keen to go anywhere they might end up some creature's lunch."

"Now, why would I even bring that up?" Nick asked.

"No reason," answered Charlie, "so don't. But some of them will. Don't mock their beliefs when they do, just keep your mouth shut as much as possible. Without them, you're stuck. You screw it up, ain't no one else going to take you out there, in which case, you're out of luck, out of a job, out of a paycheck, and out of here."

"Gotcha," Nick nodded, "anything else?"

"First person y'all gonna look up is Jean Landry. He ain't gonna talk to you, no how. Best to let Francois do the talking," said Charlie.

"Francois?" asked Nick.

"Frank; Cap'n Guidry," answered Charlie. "And that's another thing; call him Cap'n, not Captain, Skipper, Mr. Guidry, and definitely not, Francois. He hates that. I call him Frank, but that's his son's name, and he'll be along, too. He don't go nowhere without Junior. Just as well, too; that boy's as good as they come to knowing that swamp. Only his Daddy knows more about the wetlands than he does, so you'll be in good company."

"Not a problem," said Nick. "So when do we set this up?"

CLAYTON E. SPRIGGS

"Already set up," answered Dean. "They're gonna meet you tomorrow at the boat launch over by Bayou Pigeon Road. I'll pick you up early, say around six, and we'll ride out there together, so you don't get lost."

With that, the two deputies finished their beers and left. They made no mention of Nick's hanging back awhile. The men figured he had some catching up to do with his highschool sweetheart. Nick left the table and found a spot at the bar. He waited for the crowd to thin so he would get a chance to talk to Marie again. Before his chance came, he felt a sharp slap on his back and looked around in time to see a drunken Ronnie Savoy standing at his side.

"Long time no see, Nicky," Ronnie shouted out. "How's things goin'?"

"Hello, Ronnie," Nick answered.

"Sorry to hear 'bout your Mama. I heard she was a good woman. A good maid, too, as I understand it. One of my cousins used to rave 'bout what a bang-up job she did with the tile floors in her bathroom," Ronnie laughed.

"You're exactly how I remembered you," stated Nick. "Same ol' prick as in high school."

"*Coo-wee*! A prick you say?" Ronnie said with a feigned sense of indignation. "I see you still sore 'bout me stealin' your girl.

BILLY

Come on now, that be a long time ago, *couyon*. Ain't you got over that yet? Don't matter now, no how. We ain't together no more. She's a real bitch to live with; I did you a favor."

"Well *merci beaucoup*," Nick said sarcastically. "As much as I'd love to sit here and catch up on old times, I think I'm going to get going; some of us have to work in the morning. You be careful driving, Ronnie. I'd really hate to hear about anything bad happening to you."

"Same ol' Nicky," said Ronnie. "Always taking off, abandoning people. You ran out of town when Marie dumped you; you ran out on your Mama, leaving her all alone to fend for herself. Never even came to see her as she withered away over there at St. Gabriel's. Ran out on your whole city, too, when the floods came. I heard 'bout you goin' out in dem swamps to look for dem people. You hated the swamp; I'm sure you still do. I wouldn't take you out there. I'm sure you gonna jet out of there soon as there's trouble, leave everyone else to fend for themselves."

"Think what you will, Ronnie," Nick said. "Thinking was never your strong point. Yeah, I left when I had the chance. Ran all the way to college, got a degree, and then I ran all the way to the city for a career. You wouldn't know a thing about that, would you, dumbass? Some people leave, some just have others wish they would. Maybe you should ask Marie about that."

Ronnie ignored Nick's taunts. He was on a drunken roll. "I hear there's a monster creepin' 'round out there, just waiting for a tasty morsel like you to come 'round," Ronnie said with glee. "You be sure to think of me when he takes the first bite."

"I'll do that, Ronnie," answered Nick, "and I'll tell the Easter Bunny to leave you an extra chocolate egg while I'm at it, you dumb fucking *coonass*."

Ronnie stood up like he was going to throw a punch, only to slink away muttering under his breath when Nick met the challenge. Nick turned and walked toward the door, nodding to Marie on the way out. Marie nodded back, much to the dismay of Ronnie, who was sure to berate her with what was left of his drunken rage.

Marie didn't care; she was used to it. It had been the same ever since they broke up. Ronnie wasn't going to let her get on with her life as long as he could help it. With the considerable weight his family threw around the parish, it was hard to stop him. Even the sheriff and his boys weren't able to do much unless Ronnie crossed the line, and Ronnie just pushed up close to the line.

Marie sighed; such was her life, but she

BILLY

had worse things on her mind. She overheard enough to know Nick was going out in the swamp. Ronnie had been right. Nick hated the swamp. He'd be lost out there. Marie had heard the stories about the creature that was hunting people. She didn't want to believe them, but there was something going on. Everyone had been talking about it for months. Now, Nick was going right into the belly of the beast. Maybe he wasn't scared, but Marie was terrified.

CLAYTON E. SPRIGGS

Chapter Seventeen

Cap'n Guidry

Dean picked up Nick at six a.m. sharp, and they set out for the Bayou Pigeon boat launch. It was important to catch Cap'n Guidry and son early, as the two weren't going to be waiting around for any length of time for law enforcement to show up when there were important things to do. They made their life fishing and hunting for gators in the swamp, and any time wasted on dry land was money out of their pockets. When Dean and Nick showed up, the two were already preparing for the day's hunt.

"*Coo-wee*, if it ain't Deputy Dean Arceneaux!" exclaimed Cap'n Guidry.

"Cap'n," answered Dean. "Mighty fine to see you again."

CLAYTON E. SPRIGGS

The two men shook hands, and Dean nodded toward the teenager packing the boat.

"Is that the young'un?" asked Dean.

"Sure is," Guidry answered, "but not so young any more. Soon enough he be gettin' his own boat, and 'fore long, his own family to follow."

The men nodded in unison.

"So, who's your *podna*?" the Cap'n asked nodding toward Nick.

"This here is Detective Nicholas Vizier," Dean answered.

The men shook hands and introduced themselves.

"Vizier?" Guidry recollected. "I remember meeting a Vizier or two in my time. Any chance you from 'round here?"

"Yes, sir," Nick explained. "My family's been living in the area for generations. I grew up around here myself, before I went away to college."

"College?" Cap'n asked rhetorically. "Dat's good. Local college or out-of-state?"

"LSU," Nick answered with pride.

"*Coo-wee*, a tiger in our presence! Dat's good indeed. Charlie tells me you needin' a guide to help search for dose missin' kids. I gotta tell you, dey not goin' to be easy to find."

"No, sir, I suppose they ain't," Nick

BILLY

agreed. "But the way I see it, we owe it to their folks to do everything we can to bring them home."

The men nodded in silence. They appreciated the effort their fellow countrymen went to in order to help them out after the terrible storms devastated the area. The sacrifices those children made were not to be forgotten.

"According to Charlie," Guidry said, "dey got lost looking for da St. Pierre clan. Dat was dere first mistake. Even I would have a hard time finding dere place, and I been livin' here my whole life. We better start by askin' Jean Landry. His family is da closest t'ing to neighbors da St. Pierres had."

"Yep," Dean said, "that's what everyone says. Still, I doubt that Jean is going to tell us much of anything, much less take us out there. We were hoping maybe you could have a word with him."

"Yep, I reckon you right 'bout dat," Guidry replied. "No problem. We can head over dere right now. It's not too far away and, with any luck, we just might catch him 'fore he heads out for da day."

Dean excused himself, saying how he had some important errands to attend to and Cap'n Guidry instructed his boy to stay put and finish getting the boat prepared for when he returned. Nick got into Guidry's truck, and the two men headed down the road toward the Landry place. It was only a few miles up the road, and the pair arrived within minutes. Guidry instructed Nick to stay in the truck while he talked to Jean.

Nick watched as Cap'n Guidry walked up to the tidy little house and knocked. A woman came to the door and pointed around the side; then Guidry strolled around the corner where a middle-aged man in overalls and a fishing cap greeted him.

Nick saw the two men chatting amicably for a few minutes before the other man visibly tensed up and turned his back on Guidry in an effort to dismiss him. Cap'n Guidry stood his ground, awkwardly glancing toward Nick for a moment before turning back and trying to engage Jean in conversation. It looked to Nick as if the two were on the verge of a heated argument; then there was a moment of silence between them. After a brief interlude, Jean appeared to be giving the Cap'n directions before seemingly pleading with him in desperation. Guidry nodded at the man before the two parted, and the Cap'n made his way back to the truck.

"So?" Nick asked as the men drove back toward the boat launch.

"Well, just as I figured. He's not 'bout to take us out dere," Guidry replied. "He was

BILLY

adamant 'bout not wantin' us to go. He said dere was no reason. He told me he and da boy went out dere after da storm to check up on da St. Pierre's and dere wasn't a soul in sight. He hesitated a bit when he told me, and I asked him 'bout it. Den he got angry and told me he didn't want to talk 'bout it. I pressed him, and he said he saw something out dere, but wouldn't say what. He refused to talk 'bout it. I let it go, den reminded him dat dere were kids missin' out dere dat we were obligated to go look for. He said he understood, but we're just wasting our time. He said whatever is out dere, we don't want to find it, and he advised us not to go lookin' for it. I told him we had to, and he just nodded. Finally, he told me more or less how to get dere. He begged me not to go, but I guess he knows we goin' anyway."

"Do you think you'll be able to find it?" Nick asked.

"Yeah, I reckon' so," answered Guidry, "but it won't be easy. Da St. Pierres lived at some place called *Bayou Noir*, way, way deep in the swamp. Probably have to be right up on it to even see it. Still, I'm guessing we can find it sure enough. We'll have to prepare properly 'fore we head out dere. Dat is, if you still want ta go."

"I do," Nick replied. "How long before you think we'll be ready?"

"Two, t'ree days, I guess," answered Guidry. "I'll put together a list of supplies we'll need, including some dat your department will have to supply. We'll also need at least another boat, maybe two, and some help."

"Why so many?" Nick asked.

"Where we're goin' is way out dere. Whole trip might take a couple of days. Dat means more supplies, and means we'll be overnight in da swamp. Night is not a good time to be out dere, but dat's where we'll be. We'll have to be ready for anything we might come across. Dere'll be no one we can call for help if we need it. Cell phones ain't gonna work where we're goin'. Even if dey did, ain't much chance anyone's gonna find us even if dey wanted to. On top of dat, I doubt anyone's gonna be too anxious to go out dere no how. Nope, we'll be on our own."

"Yeah, I figured as much," Nick said. "What kind of supplies do you think I'll need on my end?"

"Body bags," answered Guidry. "Thick, heavy-duty body bags. If we find anything dey'll not be in da best of shape. Between da heat, da water, and da critters, dey'll be a might ripe. We ain't gonna be too happy 'bout sharing da boats with dem corpses unless we can bag 'em up tight. Might wanna bring a few extras too, just in case."

BILLY

"In case of what?" Nick asked.

Cap'n Guidry didn't answer. Their truck pulled back up to the boat launch, and the two stepped out. Guidry went back to prepare for the day's hunt before calling back over to Nick.

"One of dem boys over dere will give you a ride back to town," Guidry said, pointing to a group of amateur fisherman hanging out in the parking lot. "I'll have Frank send over a copy of da supply list so y'all can get da requisition orders. Tell Bobby I'll put together six or seven crew members on my end and a couple of boats, but he'll have to pay for it. Tell him no squabbling over da price either; it ain't gonna be cheap. Nobody's wantin' to go out dere unless dey're being properly rewarded. He'll bitch and complain, be prepared, but he'll go along with it. He ain't got no choice."

CLAYTON E. SPRIGGS

Chapter Eighteen

Preparing for the Hunt

Frank Guidry, Jr. dropped off an extensive supply list, along with a tentative itinerary and possible recruits to aid in the search. Just as Cap'n Guidry predicted, Sheriff Galliano was dismayed at the size and expense of the project. He cursed and bitched and, in the end, relented to their demands. Sheriff Bobby repeated at every opportunity how much he expected results and how Nick's job, and even career, was on the line if things didn't go as planned.

Nicholas knew that things were now officially out of his control, and no matter what the outcome, he would probably be looking for another job in the near future. Visions of his ill-fated stint in the Internal

Affairs Division over in Orleans Parish repeatedly crept into his head, and Nick tried to dismiss his feelings of impending doom as best he could. At this point, even the best outcome wasn't going to settle his nerves much. Pulling rotting corpses out of the swamp and notifying bereaved family members was always unpleasant. What the hell was he thinking, moving back home, anyway? There were multiple good reasons why he'd left in the first place, and Nick could see that there were many more that would be added to the list before long. He wondered how the weather in San Diego was at that particular moment.

The next couple of days were hectic. Requisition forms had to be filled out, corrected, refilled out, and filed. Supplies had to be acquired, including the heavy-duty body bags that were requested. That aspect of their endeavor made Nick shudder. It brought the goal of their mission into focus. They were officially searching for missing persons; unofficially, they were retrieving the bodies of dead children. With the expense and sheer effort their duties required, Nick was forced to hope that he would be bringing those bags back full. Inwardly, he prayed that he wouldn't be filling any of the 'extra' bags they were bringing along 'just in case'.

Cap'n Guidry was busy on his end, seeing

BILLY

to the supplies and recruiting boats and men to help with the search. A small number of possible searchers backed out, even with the extra hazard pay that was being offered. In the end, they procured two boats and five men, not including Cap'n Guidry, Frank, Jr., and Nicholas. It seemed like overkill to Nick to involve such a large amount of resources, but he kept his mouth shut. He was the only one of the bunch who had no experience and no business heading out into the swamp, and he knew it. Realizing that they'd be spending a night or two in the deep, dark recesses of the Atchafalaya Swamp was something that he preferred not to dwell on. Knowing that he was being surrounded with only the best and bravest of alligator hunters in the vicinity made Nick feel a measure of comfort for the time being.

Once the supplies were procured and last-minute arrangements finalized, they all agreed to leave the following morning at sunrise. The more daylight they were able to use, the less chance they would be forced to spend the night hours in the wetlands, which was preferable to everyone involved. Nick packed what few supplies he was bringing in waterproof bags and stowed them into his pack, which he intended on securing to the boat. He brought a couple of extra clips of ammo for his forty-caliber Glock that he put in a waterproof container to keep in his jacket. The handgun itself was not going to leave his side.

After going over everything twice, Nick poured himself a shot of Jack Daniels and sat back in his recliner, trying to relax enough to get at least a few hours of sleep before sunrise. He was going to need every bit of energy he had over the next few days, but even so, he knew he'd be lucky to get more than a few minutes of rest before dawn. He took another swig of his bourbon and sighed. Just what was he getting himself into? An unexpected knock at the door made him jump. Curious as to who would be coming around his place so late at night, Nick put his firearm out of sight and stumbled to the door to greet his unexpected visitor.

"Marie?" said Nick.

"Hi, Nick," Marie replied. "I'm sorry to come over here so late. If you're already in bed, I can come back another time."

"No, that's okay. Won't you come in?"

Nick stood aside to let Marie pass and then closed the door.

"Come on in. I'll pour you a drink."

Marie sat down on the sofa and fumbled nervously with her purse. Nick poured her a small glass of bourbon and sat beside her.

"So, what's on your mind?" he asked.

BILLY

"You. You're on my mind, *Boo*," answered Marie. "Ever since you came back, I've been thinking about you. To tell you the truth, I never stopped thinking about you, even from way back in high school. Oh, Nick, I'm so sorry for what I've done. I can't believe what a mess I've made of things."

"It's okay, Marie. High school was a long time ago. We've both gotten on with our lives since then."

"Yeah, well at least you have. I can't get on with mine. Ronnie won't let me. He hounds me and harasses me every chance he gets. I wish I'd never met him. And now, you're back."

"I'm back for now, Marie. There's no telling how long I'll be around before I'm out of here again. There's some truth to what Ronnie said the other night. I do have a history of abandoning those around me."

"Come on, Nick. Don't let anything Ronnie said get to you. He's just jealous of you. Always has been, always will be. No, you left because you had good reason to, just like you came back because you had to."

"I should've come back a long time ago, Marie, but I didn't. Now, I only hope it's not too late."

"Too late for what, Nick?"

Nick sat back for a moment and took another sip of his Jack Daniels. He gathered his thoughts for a moment before continuing.

"It's already too late for my mom. It's too late to keep those kids from getting lost in the swamp; maybe even too late for us."

"Too late for us?" Marie asked.

"I'm heading out in the morning to look for those kids. I'll only be gone a day or two, but depending on what I find, I might not be welcome to hang around. It'll be like finding a needle in a haystack, and I can't come back empty-handed. I'm sure I'll be shown the door in short order. Things aren't really looking good, I'll have to admit."

"I don't care about that, Nick. I just want you to come back. Hell, I don't want you to even go. It's not safe, Nick. There's something out there, something bad. I've been having nightmares thinking about you disappearing out there, or worse."

"Now, now. Don't you worry about me, Marie. There's nothing going to happen. I've been in worse places and come back without a scratch. I've faced down real dangers before, not just some made-up bullshit swamp monster. No, the worst thing that will happen to me is nothing. We'll tramp around the swamp for days without finding jack, and then it will be my ass."

"I hope you're right, Nick. I really do."

Marie sat quietly for a moment, and Nick just looked at her. She was as beautiful as he

BILLY

always remembered. He could see why it was so easy to fall in love with her back in high school and why it was so hard to fall out of love with her in the years that followed. Looking into her eyes now, he knew that he never had fallen out of love with her. He wanted her as much as he always did, and here she was. He knew he should just let it go and show her out, but he couldn't help himself. He leaned over and kissed her. She kissed him back, and they embraced with a passion that neither of them ever remembered experiencing before.

They tore at each other's clothes until they were both naked, skin against skin, each trying to consume the other with wild abandon. She straddled him as he sat on the small sofa, wrapping her arms around his shoulders and grabbing the back of his head as he buried his face into her ample breasts. She moaned as his arms held her shoulders from behind and pulled her down onto him. Their lips found each other's, and they locked on tightly as he ran his strong hands down to her quivering buttocks and squeezed them firmly as he thrust inside of her. He lifted her off the sofa, stood up as she locked her legs around his back, and then carried her to his waiting bed. He laid her on her back and fell down upon her, driving her hips further and further into the mattress while she grabbed at the wooden headboard and moaned in unyielding pleasure. Unable to contain the intensity of the moment, the two lovers climaxed and held each other's sweat-covered bodies in a tight, loving embrace.

Nick rolled over onto his back, Marie laying her head upon his chest as they both panted fiercely, trying to catch their breaths. He tenderly stroked her long, brown hair and stared into the darkness, trying to hold on to the moment and never let it go. Soft tears silently ran down Marie's cheeks as she listened to her lover's heart beat in unison with hers. After a few quiet moments, Nick felt the dripping of Marie's tears on his chest.

"Are you crying?" he gently asked.

Marie lay in silence for awhile before answering, "Just a little."

"Why, what's wrong?"

"Oh, Nick. I don't want you to go."

"Hey, hey, I'm not going anywhere."

"I mean, I don't want you to go out there tomorrow. I'm scared."

"Marie, there's nothing to be scared about. I'll be alright."

"You don't understand. I know you don't believe in these things. Normally, neither do I. But I have a bad feeling about it. I can't explain it, but I just know there's something out there. I, I love you, Nick."

There, she had said it. She knew there

BILLY

was no retreating, no taking it back. Marie didn't care. She didn't care what Ronnie or anyone else had to say about it, either. The only thing she cared about now was Nick. She waited in silence, hoping he would say the words she longed to hear.

"I love you, too, Marie. I always have, I always will. So don't you worry. If I ever had a reason to come back home, I do now. There is nothing, and I mean nothing, that's going to keep me from coming back, coming back to you. You believe me, don't you?"

"Yes, of course I believe you, and I hope you're right. I'm probably just being silly. It's just that I've never felt like this about anyone before, and I need you to come back to me. I shouldn't be talking like this to you. You have enough on your mind. Just forget I said anything, but come back to me. I need you."

"I need you, too, Marie, and don't worry. There's nothing in the world that's going to keep me away from you."

Nick kissed her forehead before drifting off to sleep. Marie lay quietly next to him, listening to the rhythm of his breathing and the steady beating of his heart, hoping that he was right. She stared into the night and tried to suppress her fears. As tired as she was, Marie fought against the inevitability of sleep. With sleep, came the nightmares – the terrible visions of sharp claws and pointed teeth, of hungry red eyes burning with hatred, staring into her soul from out of the darkness of the Atchafalaya.

PART THREE

ATCHAFALAYA

CLAYTON E. SPRIGGS

Chapter Nineteen

Down the Bayou

The following morning came too early. Nick had the sensation that he'd just closed his eyes for a brief moment when the unwelcome sound of his alarm clock woke him up to the unpleasant reality of daybreak. Marie was lying next to him, quietly mumbling in her sleep, apparently in the midst of a bad dream. Given the grave conversation the two shared the previous night, Nick didn't have to guess what it was about. He took a deep breath, resigning himself to the task awaiting him, and rolled out of bed, trying not to disturb her.

He was dressed, packed, and headed down the road in his truck as the sun began to rise. By the time he pulled into the parking lot of the boat launch, Nick could see that the rest of the men were already preparing for the search. Four men that he'd never met before were busy loading gear and provisions into two boats. Another man Nick didn't recognize was helping Deputy Doucet unload the requested infamous body bags from the back of an official SUV. Nicholas parked his truck, grabbed his gear, and headed toward the group, nodding to Charlie on the way. Cap'n Guidry and son walked over from the bait shop, stopping by the deputy's truck to double-check the supply list and sign a few last-minute forms.

"Morning, Cap'n, Charlie," Nick said.

"Good morning to you, Nick," Charlie said in return. "You ready?"

"As ready as I'm going to be," answered Nick.

"Don't you worry none, Detective," Guidry said. "You in good hands. We got da best swamp rats in da parish gonna help us with da search. Come on, I'll introduce you to da crew."

Nick followed Guidry and son to where the other men were gathered, and introductions were made. A tall, burly man with a deep, dark tan named Henry Trahan shook his hand first, almost breaking his bones with a vice-like grip while smiling innocently. Next up was an even bigger giant named Joseph Batiste, whose long, gray, scraggly hair and goatee made him look like an insane biker.

BILLY

Nick was prepared this time for the pissing contest of firm handshakes and almost felt let down when the man just fist-bumped him. Kirk Alleman, a middle-aged man with a permanent squint in his eyes, shook his hand next. The rough-looking older man didn't say much, preferring to nod before turning his head to the side and spitting a stream of tobacco-laced saliva onto the white shells of the parking lot. Nick noticed the man's worn-out brown baseball cap spelled out the Cajun equivalent of big oil: *Texaceaux*. Last to round out the men in the second boat was an almost emaciated looking man named Dennis LeFleur. On closer inspection, Nick could see that Dennis was surprisingly strong and healthy and had likely been thin and gangly since birth.

Kenneth Nunez, a young man who looked to be in his early twenties, was the last of the men to accompany the group. He had longish brown hair and a goatee, and he wore some kind of designer sunglasses. Nick later found out that he was the older brother of one of Frank Guidry, Jr.'s high school buddies and he'd be riding along with Nick and the Cap'n and son in the lead boat.

The crew finished loading the boats and set out while the day was still young. It was a long ride out to where they figured the St. Pierre cabin was, and none of the men wished to prolong the trip that far into the swamp any longer than necessary. They made good time early in the day, sticking to the larger rivers and *bayous* whenever they could. By the early afternoon, their luck ran out. Forced into navigating the smaller and less-traveled waterways as they rode deeper into the swamp, they ran into patches of hyacinths that blocked their way. Several times, they had to backtrack and find alternative routes, which made their search for such an elusive destination more difficult.

The men were well versed in the difficulties of traveling through the swamp and took it in stride. They'd seen it all before. Nick seemed to be the only one who had misgivings about getting lost, and he kept them to himself. The sheriff's office paid handsomely for the experience of the search party, and Nick was grateful, knowing that he'd be hopelessly lost even this early into the expedition if left to his own devices.

He couldn't help but think how foolish it was for those kids to go out there by themselves in the first place. Even with the experience of those around him, Nick would have preferred to be anywhere else than where he was at the moment. He shuddered to think how terrified those young volunteers must've been when their dire situation became all too real. St. Elizabeth's Institute

BILLY

for the Mentally Ill seemed to be the obvious destination for anyone hopelessly lost in the swamp for any length of time alone, and even that was only marginally preferable to the morgue.

"I can see why old man Landry didn't wanna come out here," Cap'n Guidry stated to no one in particular. "What I can't understand is why dem St. Pierres stayed out here in da first place. Dis place is way passed Bum Fucked Egypt and at least two hundred miles from nowhere."

"*Ca viens?*" shouted Trahan from the other boat. "How's it going?"

"No worries, *podna*," Guidry replied. "According to Landry, we be dere soon enough."

About an hour later, they came across a thick grove of cypress trees. The crew slowed the boats down and sailed cautiously down the small waterway, carefully making their way around the cypress knots, or *boscoyo*, which impeded their path. The water turned brackish and the sky grew dark as a large thundercloud temporarily blocked the sunlight. No one made a sound, and Nick felt the hair on his neck stand up.

"Hear dat?" Cap'n Guidry asked.

"I don't hear a t'ing," Frank, Jr. replied.

"Dat's what I mean. Awfully quiet," the Cap'n replied.

"Dis ain't natural," Dennis said from the other boat. "Ain't supposed to be dis quiet out here. I ain't never seen dis before."

"Hush up now, you *Skinny Mullet*," Batiste stated in his deep baritone. "You sounding *motier foux*, half crazy."

"Quiet! That's enough, you two," said Henry.

They drifted slowly down the *bayou*, those in the front watching for the lilies and stumps rising out of the black water, while the rest of the men scanned the horizon for any sign that they were in the right place.

"*Coo-wee*! Will ya look at dat?" Cap'n Guidry exclaimed at last.

In front of them, barely visible behind the cypress trees and Spanish moss, was a small, wooden shack perched precariously on wooden poles sticking out of the brackish water. There was only a dark opening where the front door must've been and a large hole in the tin roof. Random debris was scattered around the brush and small mounds of dirt that surrounded the cabin. On the front of the house, painted with bright red spray paint, was a symbol that was familiar to the group.

BILLY

"I t'ink we're dere. Detective Nick, on behalf of Cap'n Guidry and the Swamp Rats, I welcome you to *Bayou Noir*."

CLAYTON E. SPRIGGS

Chapter Twenty

Bayou Noir

The boats drifted slowly up to the dock in front of the cabin and tied to the wooden posts. The men were quiet, and Nick could feel tension in the air, a sensation that surprised him amongst a crew that grew up in the swamp and were so seemingly familiar with its environment. He noticed what a watchful eye the others had on their surroundings, feeling himself growing increasingly pensive in the process. If the self-described swamp rats felt uncomfortable being there, Nick reasoned, something was definitely amiss at *Bayou Noir*.

"Frank, you stay here with da boats," Cap'n Guidry instructed his son, "and keep an eye out."

The younger Guidry seemed annoyed at having been singled out amongst the crew. As creepy as the cabin was, he was dying to see what was inside. The thought of staying back alone didn't make him feel any safer.

"Keep an eye out for what?" he asked.

"For anything dat don't belong," answered the Cap'n.

The elder Guidry led the crew up the wooden deck and inspected the outside of the cabin and the cryptic message painted on the rotting boards out front.

"Looks like dem kids were here, alright," Guidry said. "Or, at least, someone was after da storm. Wanna explain dis to us, Detective?"

"It was them, alright," answered Nick. "The initials, *GM*, stand for Generation Millennium, which is what they called themselves."

"What kind of a stupid name is that?" Kenny asked.

"Dat from someone who calls demselves a Swamp Rat," Joe Batiste sarcastically replied.

Nick ignored the others and continued with his translation. "The date at the top is self-explanatory, and the *WA* to the right probably stands for wild animals or some such warning. That's the spot where the hazards are listed, such as *GL* for gas leaks,

BILLY

et cetera, but there isn't a standard way to write whatever you may come across. Judging from the date up top and the surroundings, I'm sure wild animals is what you'd expect to find around a group of dead..., well, you know."

They looked at the *4DB* painted in red at the bottom of the X and nodded in silence. No explanation was needed. Whatever was left of the St. Pierre family after the WA's got to them was found by Generation Millennium back in September; any further questions the Swamp Rats needed answering, they were going to have to get for themselves.

Without another word, Nick walked into the darkness of the cabin, followed by the rest of the men. They made their way slowly, letting their eyes adjust to the poor lighting of the dank, stuffy cabin.

The place was a mess. By the water line near the ceiling, they could see that the entire first floor had been flooded during the storm. The force of the water and sludge it left in its wake destroyed any sense of order in the small confines of the tiny, wooden shack. Mud and moldy green residue covered everything. The smell was awful, and the majority of the men covered their noses and mouths with whatever cloth they had with them. Flies and other insects buzzed about, feasting on the disgusting smorgasbord of rotting things.

"*Merde*!" shouted Dennis as he sprang from his spot and almost fell over a rocking chair that was lying on its side.

The group jumped from the sudden outburst just in time to see a sizeable water moccasin slither out from under a pile of unrecognizable refuse. Kirk and Henry casually stepped to the side as the poisonous reptile glided past them and out the front door. Once the black snake dropped into the murky water out front, the crew got back to the task at hand.

"*Coo-wee*!" exclaimed Cap'n Guidry. "I t'ink we found one of da family."

On the floor at the Cap'n's feet, amongst the slimy remains of the family's belongings, a human ribcage was visible. Next to what was left of the poor victim's torso, a skull and a few assorted bones, some still with remnants of flesh attached, lay scattered about. The internal organs of the deceased were almost nonexistent, either rotted away in the hot, humid climate, or eaten by the abundant assortment of scavengers in the area. The men looked on in reverent silence for a moment before scanning the rest of the cabin for the remainder of the ill-fated family.

"Here's another one," Henry stated,

BILLY

pointing at the floor near a hole in the wall where a window had once been. "It's in no better shape than the other one."

"*Cho! Co!*" Kenny exclaimed from the back room. "Now this don't make no sense."

The men walked toward the back and stared down at the sight before them. In the small back room of the cabin was a bed, and resting on it was the decaying remains of what appeared to be a middle-aged woman. Unlike the other two bodies, this one had been placed on the bed and left mostly undisturbed by the scavengers that had done so much damage to the others.

"What the fuck?" Nick asked to no one in particular.

The men looked to each other without a word. No one had any plausible theories to explain the unexpected sight, so none were offered. The group wandered back into the main room of the house when Dennis LeFleur noticed something overhead.

"Looks like da door to da attic," he said, pointing to a small, square wooden frame on the ceiling. "Wonder why dey didn't just go up dere?"

Nick shuddered, remembering the story Margaret told while she was under hypnosis.

"Dat is da question of da day, gentlemen," Guidry said. "Guess we gonna find out."

They looked around and found a ladder

amongst the garbage strewn about the floor. Once it was inspected and found sound enough for use, the men placed it under the small opening overhead. The crew looked at one another, but everyone kept their eyes averted and none made any move toward the ladder.

"Well, they had the ladder here, so surely they intended to go up there, unless it was left here by those kids," Nick stated. "The sign up front said there were four dead bodies; there were four members of the St. Pierre family that were known to be here during the storm. I guess we'll find another one up there."

Nick instinctively checked his firearm by his side, took a deep breath, and headed up the ladder. He pushed the small, wooden door to the side, and he could see there was a moderate amount of light in the hot space overhead, undoubtedly due to the holes in the tin roof caused by the ferocity of the storm.

Nick poked his head up through the opening and scanned the area. He drew back quickly and almost threw up. The others looked at him with a combination of dread, curiosity, and anticipation, but Nick didn't say a word. He took a few deep breaths and climbed up the ladder, disappearing into the hidden space above.

BILLY

On the dusty boards at his feet, not far from the small opening to the cabin below, lay the body of Poppie St. Pierre. The sight was repulsive, even to an experienced investigator like Nick. The poor victim was bloated from the noxious gasses and microscopic organisms that ate at him from the inside and was ripped to pieces by the birds that had feasted on him from the outside. His eyes were missing, as was most of his flesh, and his intestines were strewn about the dusty floorboards of the attic. Nick could see that the man's throat had been ripped apart by sharp claws, a sight that was incongruent with the remains of the rest of the man's family.

It had been months since the two storms had ravaged the area, meaning an exact cause of death would be all but impossible even for the most skilled coroner to determine. Under these circumstances, in this place, with what they had discovered so far, Nick could see that even Sherlock Holmes would be baffled.

The two bodies below lie scattered on the floor, both victims could have drowned in the flood, then been ravaged by the elements; another below may have drowned, yet was somehow placed gingerly on a bed after the waters subsided by who knows, and for what reason. Nick figured that the original search party might have moved some of the remains around, but he knew this wouldn't really explain it. The woman's body in the back room must've been moved there right after the storm for it to remain in the shape in which they had found it. By the time Generation Millennium came here, it would've been too late. And now, there was this body in the attic.

Nick scanned the area around him and made mental notes of all that he surveyed. A shotgun lay near the corpse and a spent shell was on the floor nearby. A giant puddle of dried blood surrounded the body, and Nick could see various markings throughout the floorboards. Most of the prints appeared to be from birds, most likely crows, although none were of good enough quality to be sure. Nick noticed a few larger prints that resembled the claws of a much larger predator, though he had no idea what could have made such markings. Upon closer inspection, there appeared to be six fingers and/or toes on each paw, but it was impossible to determine exactly. As far as Nick knew, there wasn't a creature on Earth that would leave such a mark.

"Fucking swamp monster," he whispered to himself and shuddered at the thought.

Nick knew the others were impatiently waiting below for his return, so he glanced

BILLY

once more around the attic before heading for the opening at his feet. The remainder of the small area was empty, so he started down the ladder, before stopping himself. In the far corner, almost hidden in the shadows, Nick noticed a pile of iron chains. One end looked to be wrapped around and fastened to a wooden post, the other end held an empty shackle.

"What the hell?" he muttered to himself before resuming his way down the ladder. When Nick met the other men, he could see some kind of explanation was in order.

"The other body's up in the attic," he said. "Probably Poppie St. Pierre. My guess is that the body in the back is his wife and these two up front are the kids. There's no sign of the search party we're looking for, though surely they were here by the sign out front."

"Why didn't the rest of the family go up in the attic?" Kenny asked.

Nick remained silent; he had no explanation – at least he had no explanation that made any sense. He could see there was a reason, a good reason, a big, scary, good reason to not go up there, but he had no way to explain it and didn't want to try. It really didn't matter now, he figured. Whatever it was that the family had chained up there wasn't up there anymore. He wanted to forget all of that now and get the hell out of there.

They needed to find those kids, or whatever was left of them, and then go home. He didn't get paid enough to hunt down the boogeyman. In any event, the kids had been there, and then they left and got lost. That's what Margaret had said, and Nick was finding himself believing her crazy story more than he cared to.

St. Elizabeth's wasn't a place he wanted to call home, and he had no intention of finding himself interned there for any length of time when this was all over. No, he told himself, not going to do it. We're just going to stick to the mission and fuck everything else. Don't know, don't care what the fuck was up in the attic, and don't want to find out.

"Let's get the body bags and get these poor people out of here," Nick instructed. "They deserve a proper funeral."

Kenny and Dennis headed out the door with Kirk trailing behind them. After a few minutes, Kirk popped his head back through the front door and addressed the elder Guidry, "Cap'n, you need to get out here."

Guidry walked out front, followed by the rest.

"What da hell?" he asked. "Where da hell dat boy gone off to?"

The boats sat empty out by the dock. There was no sign of the younger Guidry.

BILLY

"Frank! Frank!" the men began to shout, scanning the horizon. "Where you at?"

There was no sign of the boy anywhere.

"Maybe he gone off to take a piss or something," offered Joseph Batiste.

"He'd be back by now," Henry answered. "Somethin's not right."

They fanned out and searched around the cabin, looking for the lost boy.

"Nick, come see," Kenny said quietly so the others couldn't hear.

Nick walked over to the boat where Frank had been seen last and looked down at where Kenny was pointing. A few splatters of fresh blood could be seen on the side of the boat, but nothing else.

"What do you make of that?" Kenny asked.

"Not sure, but it ain't good," Nick replied.

"When Cap'n sees this, he ain't gonna be none too pleased," Kenny said.

Nope, that he's not, thought Nick.

The men slowly made their way back toward the boats, and Nick could see the near panic in Cap'n Guidry's eyes. Nick knew once the man saw the blood all hell was going to break loose, but saw no way to avoid it. No, they all needed to see it, and they all needed to keep their heads together, or things would only go from bad to worse.

"Cap'n," Nick said evenly, "you need to see something."

Kenny held his tongue and looked at his feet while Nick showed Guidry and the rest of the crew the blood marks on the side of the boat.

"Could be from da bait," Guidry stated, not truly believing his own words.

"EEEEEEEEaaaaaaaaaaaagggggghhhhhhhh!!!!"

The roar tore through the silent air and ripped into the hearts of the Swamp Rats.

"*Pic kee moi*! Fuck me!" Henry shouted in surprise.

"What da hell was dat?" Kirk exclaimed, swallowing some of his chewing tobacco by mistake.

"Whatever it is, it ain't too far away," said Joe.

They all peered in the direction they determined the sound had come from, then back toward Cap'n Guidry. Nick noticed the man's teeth were clenched in anger, and his face was beginning to turn red.

"Get in da boats and grab da rifles," he stated. "We got huntin' to do."

Chapter Twenty-One

Tracking the Beast

The men gathered their firearms and started off in the direction that the unholy sound had come from. They made their way carefully down the overgrown waterway, keeping a keen eye on their surroundings for any sign of the missing Guidry or the beast that took him. Cap'n remained silent, his face tense with worry and anger and his hands tightly clutching the shotgun in his grasp as his eyes relentlessly scanned the horizon. When the boats rounded a sharp bend in the *bayou*, a large patch of water lilies rose in front of them, impeding their progress.

"Cut dem motors," instructed Cap'n. "Get dem propellers out of da water; we gonna paddle tru so's we don't get stuck."

The crew was already on the task; with the exception of Nick, they were all experienced with navigating through the wetlands. It was not uncommon to find patches of hyacinths or downed trees that could make traveling through the smaller waterways difficult, especially this far into the swamp. Normally, one would go around these obstacles whenever possible, but there was nothing normal in what the men were doing now.

Pushing through the overgrowth was tedious, but eventually the boats made it out onto open water again. While the men in the back of the boats dropped the motors back into the water in preparation to regain momentum, the others watched carefully down the *bayou* for any indication that they were heading in the right direction.

"Look over dere," Kirk said, pointing to a small patch of mud sticking out of the water between some cypress trees.

A small bush swayed gently back and forth, as though blown by the wind. None of the men could detect a breeze at the moment. Something had been there moments before, watching them. Whatever it was, it was still nearby.

"Y'all stay back a little," Cap'n told the men in the second boat, "and keep a sharp

BILLY

eye out. We're gonna have a closer look."

Guidry guided the boat slowly up to the spot between the trees, and Kenny tied it off to one of the *boscoyo* nearby. Once Nick convinced himself that there was nothing within arm's reach that could grab him unexpectedly, he holstered his handgun and hopped out of the boat to inspect the area. Cap'n Guidry followed him onto a small patch of soggy dirt, while Kenny stayed behind, his hunting rifle poised for action.

"See anything?" Nick asked.

"Hmmm," Guidry mumbled, "somet'ing was here. Not sure what."

Nick looked down to where Guidry was pointing and saw fresh claw marks in the muddy earth. He had a sense of déjà vu at the sight of six toes per print, but kept himself in check. Nick could feel sweat pour down the back of his neck and instinctively reached for his Glock as he quickly scanned the immediate vicinity for any sign of danger. Guidry noticed the detective's reaction, but kept quiet for the moment.

"We better get back in da boat," he said. "We wastin' time just standin' around."

Nick wasn't about to argue and happily complied with Cap'n's order. Kenny untied the boat, and they drifted back to where the others sat waiting for them.

"See anything?" asked Joe.

"Somet'ing was dere," answered Cap'n. "Left some fresh tracks in da mud. Not sure what it was, but have an idea it might be what we after."

"Eeeeeeeaaaaaagggghhhhh!"

The crew jumped at the unexpected, terrifying shriek.

"*Cho! Co!*" Kenny exclaimed. "What the fuck was that?"

"It sounded like it coming from over there," Henry stated, pointing to an area just beyond sight down the *bayou*.

"Let's go," Guidry stated.

The men fired up the engines and cruised down the narrow waterway in the direction of the terrible roar. They had their guns out and ready to fire at whatever they encountered, but no one saw a thing. After a little while, they were forced to cut the engines and stop the boats, their way blocked once again by an overgrowth of vegetation.

"*Voila merde!*" cursed Henry. "Not again."

"Detective," Joe said, "you see dat?"

Nick saw. Everyone saw. The circles of green lilies jetting up out of the water in front of them were covered with patches of sticky, red liquid – blood – most likely Frank, Jr.'s blood.

"*Fils de pute!* Son of a bitch!" Kirk stated before spitting a huge glob of tobacco laden

BILLY

saliva over the side of the boat.

"*Coo-wee*! Over dere!" Dennis exclaimed, pointing toward the moss covered trees up ahead.

The men looked up, only to see an empty space amongst the shadows.

"There's nothing there, *Skinny Mullet*," Henry said.

"Dere was something dere a minute ago. I saw it," protested Dennis.

"What did you see?" asked Joe.

"I saw....I don't know," answered Dennis.

"You don't know what you saw?" asked Henry.

"It don't matter what I saw. I saw somet'ing. It was dere. It's still here, somewhere," Dennis replied.

"And how you know dat?" Joe asked.

"'Cause it's quiet, too quiet," Dennis said. "Just like back at dat house. Dere's somet'ing out here dat don't belong. You all know what I'm talkin' about, even if ya don't wanna say it."

"*Tuat t'en grosse bueche*! Shut your big mouth, *couyon*!" Cap'n said. "Dis ain't no time for children stories. Henry, y'all go have a look see, and be careful. We stay out here dis time, but no worries, anything come creepin' gonna get blasted real quick."

Henry guided his boat up to the spot where Dennis indicated. Kirk dropped the anchor over the side and followed Joe onto the stretch of dirt under the trees. Henry and Dennis stayed in the boat and kept watch. After a few minutes, the two men returned and they made their way back to where the others waited.

"See anyt'ing?" Cap'n Guidry asked.

"Just some gator tracks," Joe said.

"Dat's bullshit," interrupted Dennis. "It ain't no gator I saw. Gators don't stand up when dey walk."

Before Joseph could reply, Kirk chimed in, "I hate to say it, but Dennis is right. Dem tracks weren't made by no gator."

"How you know that?" Kenny asked.

"'Cause ain't no gator I ever seen got six toes," replied Kirk.

Cap'n Guidry looked at Nick.

"You know some t'ing, dontcha, Detective?" Guidry asked. "I t'ink it's time you told us what was in dat attic."

Chapter Twenty-Two

Qui C'est q' Ca?

Nick took a deep breath, trying to gather his thoughts for a moment before speaking. He didn't want to tell the others what he was thinking. Hell, he wasn't even sure what his thoughts were anymore.

There was one thing he knew, he didn't want to spook the rest of the crew into abandoning the mission. It was bad enough Frank, Jr. had disappeared. There was no way they were going to just let that go. But Nick had been sent out there to find the kids missing from the search party, and he had every intention of seeing it through, Frank or no Frank, monster or no monster. Nick knew if he showed back up empty handed, he would be looking for a new job, a new place to live, and a new girlfriend. He hadn't come this far to give up now.

"The only thing up in that attic was Poppie St. Pierre's rotting corpse," Nick said at last.

"Da only t'ing?" Dennis asked. "I find dat hard to believe."

"Believe what you want, it's the truth," Nick said firmly.

"We seen tracks just like y'all seen," Cap'n Guidry stated. "Six toes on each. See any t'ing like dat up in dat attic, Detective?"

"Yeah, maybe," Nick said. "It was hard to tell. The body wasn't in the best of shape."

"The ones downstairs probably drowned, I'd say. Don't even want to guess how the one in the back got there," said Henry. "What happened to the one in the attic?"

"No telling," Nick answered. "Like I said, the body wasn't in the best of shape."

"I'm guessing he didn't drown, d'oh," Cap'n said. "Ain't dat right, Detective?"

"No, I'm guessing he didn't drown," answered Nick.

"You seen anyt'ing else up dere dat might explain dis?" asked Guidry.

"There were some chains."

"Chains?" asked Joe. "Why was dere chains? What was in dem?"

"Nothing," answered Nick. "At least, not anymore."

BILLY

"*Ga-lee*! Dem stories be true!" Dennis said. "We best get out of here whilst we can; it gonna be dark soon."

"We ain't goin' nowheres!" Cap'n said. "Not without Frank."

"I hate to say it, Cap'n, but you know as well as the rest of us, Frank is gone," Henry said.

"*Pic kee toi*! Fuck you!" Guidry said between clenched teeth. He lowered his gun, tightening his grip on the firearm, and said to everyone present, "We ain't leavin' my boy out here. We gonna find him and we gonna kill dat t'ing dat took him. Any of you got a problem with dat, you gonna have a problem with me."

No one said a word. The Swamp Rats averted their eyes from Cap'n's angry glare and situated themselves to continue the search. Nick looked down at the body bags at his feet and shuddered – 'just in case' indeed. Now wasn't the time to remind everyone of what they were here for, what they were getting paid to do. Instead, he kept his mouth shut, opened his eyes, and looked toward the horizon, and hoped against hope that things would start looking up.

The afternoon wore on, and the light began to dim as the sky became covered with dark clouds. After awhile, it began to drizzle. Everyone thought it would be a good idea to head in and try to find some shelter before the sun set and the weather got rougher – everyone but Cap'n Guidry. He just sat stoically in the back of the boat, one hand on the rudder and the other one clutching his shotgun. The Swamp Rats resigned themselves to their unwelcome fate. The only place they were heading was further into the swamp.

"Cap'n," said Kenny as they glided past a thick grove of cypress trees, "there's some markings on the trees."

The crew inspected the vegetation as they passed and saw what Kenny was referring to. Scratched onto the trees at various places, they could see sharp claw marks indented into the bark.

"Just like a bear makes," Nick said.

"'Cept that wasn't no bear dat made dose," Dennis said.

"Dumb beast fucked up," Cap'n stated. "Now we know where he's headed."

It was difficult, if not impossible, to track an animal through the swamp, even for those as experienced as the Swamp Rats. Land was scarce and only rose above the surface of the water in patches sporadically. The water was dark and thick with sediment and teeming with snakes and other unsavory creatures. Mosquitoes and flies swarmed everywhere, sucking the blood of their

BILLY

victims indiscriminately and spreading disease. Spiders, snakes, and worse lurked seen and unseen within striking distance at all times. The oppressive heat smothered the group, causing sweat to soak into their clothes, the sticky residue acting like glue for the putrid aroma of male body odor mixed with rotting vegetation and stagnant water.

Without clearly discernible landmarks and with the meandering *bayous* that became impassable at regular intervals, it was all one could do to not get lost. The crew was so far into the swamp, they were now in uncharted territory. With the steady drizzle that only threatened to get worse and the few hours of daylight quickly fading, the desperation of the men was increasing by the minute. When it looked like all hope of finding their way was lost, they came across the markings. Now, all they had to do was let the beast's own mistake be his downfall. Things were beginning to look up.

The crew drifted carefully through the swamp, navigating the narrow streams and *bayous* while keeping a watchful eye on their surroundings and their fingers on the triggers of their guns. When it seemed as though the sky was going to dump a torrent of precipitation on the men, the rain suddenly abated. A bright flash of sunlight lit up the swamp, shining down through the leaves and Spanish moss overhead and giving everything around them a warm glow. A slight breeze broke through the oppressive, stagnant air. An unspoken sense of relief was felt amongst the crew, and everyone began to breathe a little easier for the first time since they came across the creepy shack hidden amongst the trees. After a few pleasant moments, as if on cue, the men became aware of the deathly silence that engulfed their environment. Before a word could be spoken, a familiar, but terrifying, roar broke the silence.

"Eeeeeeaaaaaaagggghhhhhh!"

"*Merde*'!" Dennis shouted. "Dat t'ing scares da shit out of me every time."

"It came from back dere," Joe said, pointing to a patch of overgrown swamp grass.

"We got it now," said Cap'n. "Henry, y'all go 'round toward da right. Go quiet now, nice and easy. We gonna go down dat way to da left. We gonna make a bit of noise to distract it some. When da time comes, everyone blast away. Just remember to aim low; we don't wanna catch each other in da crossfire. Ain't no hospitals out here. Any of us do somethin' stupid and get shot, we'll be using one of dese bags Nick brought along."

The men sprung into action. Hunting came naturally to the Swamp Rats, as they'd

BILLY

done it successfully since they were young children. At last, the tables were turned. They had the creature cornered, outnumbered, and grossly out-armed. It was time for justice; it was time for vengeance.

Before long, the boats were in position. Cap'n Guidry suddenly hollered out, causing Nick to almost drop his Glock overboard. Gunfire erupted, breaking the unholy silence of the swamp with a relenting explosion of artificial thunder. After what seemed like an eternity, the firing stopped.

Smoke filled the air and the small patch of vegetation looked like it had been chewed up and spit out by an industrial turbine of monumental proportions. The men looked on, not knowing what to expect. Nothing stirred amongst the shredded swamp grass on the small mound of mud. The men cautiously approached, each boat from opposite sides, until they were upon the site of the carnage.

"I don't see nothin'," Dennis said.

"There's nothin' here," agreed Kenny.

"Wait. There's blood," Nick said, pointing to a small area barely visible below the surface of the water.

Joe reached over with a long, metal pole, and hooked onto a batch of unrecognizable flesh, pulling it to the side of the boat. He reached down and turned the floating object over as the crew looked on in horror. A disfigured face became distinguishable amongst the torn flesh and blood bobbing up and down in the filthy water.

"Frank," muttered Joe.

"*Oo ye yi*!" shouted Cap'n Guidry, tears filling his eyes. "My boy! What you done to my boy, *feet pue tan*! You goddamned son of a bitch!"

A loud clap of thunder erupted overhead, and rain came crashing down upon the mournful group. The sky darkened from the sudden cloud cover, and they all knew what was left of the sun was rapidly sinking beyond the horizon. Soon, night would be upon them, and they'd be forced to face down the beast in the dark. The feelings of sadness, anger, and desperation enveloped the men as they became drenched in the downpour and the boats began to fill with rainwater.

"Eeeeeeeaaaaaagghhhh!"

The unwelcome roar called to the crew from a distance even further into the swamp. It struck into the hearts of the men, hitting each where they hurt the most. Cap'n Guidry felt what was left of his heart split into shards of broken glass, ripping into his soul and filling him with loss and hatred. To the rest of the Swamp Rats, their chests beat wildly with fear and dread. The nightmares

BILLY

of their childhood came bursting to the surface, filling their distraught minds with visions of big teeth and sharp claws.

"Eeeeeeeaaaaaaagggghhhh!"

To Nick, the sound left a feeling indescribable. He remembered the outlandish story he heard from the crazy girl in the insane asylum. A story too ridiculous to be true. Memories of monsters smiling with flesh-covered fangs.

"Eeeeeeeaaaaaaagggghhhh!"

"Almost sounds like it's laughing at us," Nick mumbled under his breath before catching himself. He turned around to see if Guidry had heard his unfortunate remark, and saw the old man's face filled with determination and hatred. Nick shuddered and turned away. There was no image of any swamp creature that was as filled with terror and impending doom as the one on the man behind him. He glanced over to see Dennis looking at him from the next boat.

"Qui c'est q 'ca?" he asked, his voice broken with fear. "What is dat t'ing?"

CLAYTON E. SPRIGGS

Chapter Twenty-Three

Hopeless

As the last of that fateful day's light faded, the crew pulled the battered remains of Frank Guidry, Jr. into the boat and zipped him up in one of the sturdy black body bags. He had been ripped apart by sharp claws and further ravaged by vile insects while submerged in the filthy swamp water. Everyone was grateful that Sheriff Galliano's office provided the airtight bags. Frank's remains were getting ripe in the hot and humid environment and toxic for his neighbors in the boat.

Cap'n Guidry ordered the men to anchor down in an open area for the night so that they'd be able to keep a watchful eye out for the return of the beast. It was a miserable situation to be in. There was no shelter from the intermittent rainfall, and the waves kept the boats rocking just enough to prevent any relaxation on the part of the passengers. The men officially took turns keeping watch, although, in truth, none of them were able to rest. The Swamp Rats sat quietly through the night, wet and afraid.

Cap'n Guidry sat in the puddle of putrid water at the bottom of the small boat with Frank, Jr.'s body bag on his lap, his hushed sobbing barely audible to the others. The anguish of losing his only son was almost unbearable and the sense of loss was shared by his friends, many of whom knew the younger Guidry since the child was born. Tears mixed with raindrops on the cheeks of the men in the two boats; fear and hatred tore into their souls.

"Eeeeeaaaaaaggghhhhhh!"

The roar of the beast echoed from a patch of cypress and tupelo trees to the right of the group. The men cast their flashlights in the direction from which the sound had erupted and steadied their firearms, but nothing further was seen or heard. Time wore on, and the crew sat back and listened, watched, and waited.

"Eeeeeeaaaaaaaagggghh!"

This time, the terrifying shriek emanated from their left and seemed further away.

BILLY

Once again, the Swamp Rats shone their lights in the general direction of the beast's roar and watched and waited. Again, no further disruption ensued.

"*Co faire?*" asked Dennis. "Why is dat t'ing torturing us?"

"It's fucking with us, *Skinny Mullet*," answered Henry. "*Fils de pute* t'inks we playin' some kind of game."

"If it's a game, he's winnin'," muttered Kirk before spitting a glob of brown saliva over the side of the boat.

"*Tuat t'en grosse bueche!*" Guidry said, his voice filled with anger. "Dis ain't no game, and dat t'ing ain't winnin' shit. *Je vas te passé une calotte*, I'm gonna pass a slap at your ass next time I hear you sayin' any t'ing like dat again."

"He didn't mean nothin' by it," said Joe. "We all grieving with you, Cap'n, you know dat. When daylight comes, we gonna bring justice to dat t'ing out dere. I swear by it."

Guidry nodded; nothing else needed to be said. Occasionally throughout the rest of the night, the roar of the beast could be heard. It came from all directions, sometimes close, but mostly from further and further away. By dawn, nothing could be heard but the sounds of the frogs and birds around them.

The new day was upon them, and as the light returned and the mist evaporated, the crew set out once again in search of the creature that mercilessly attacked them and mocked them in their anguish throughout the night.

The Swamp Rats started again where they had left off, following the claw marks on the trees until the markings were no longer visible. After that, they meandered down whatever streams and *bayous* they came across, stopping from time to time to look for tracks in the wet mud whenever they could. By noon, the crew found themselves back to where they'd began, without a clue as to which direction they came from or in which to proceed.

"Dis be a waste of time," Dennis stated. "We're no further along den when we started out."

"It's hopeless," Kenny agreed. "We have no idea of where that t'ing is."

"We ain't giving up," Cap'n Guidry said. "I don't care what y'all say. I'll find dat t'ing if it's da last t'ing I do."

"It may be, at this rate," Kenny said.

"Don't you be gettin' smart with me, boy!" Cap'n said.

Nick could see things were falling apart. He knew that the majority of the men were looking to give up and go home, and he couldn't really blame them. In any event, it appeared that none of them present, save

BILLY

himself, had any intention of looking for the lost search party. Nick was the only one left who'd remembered why they'd come out there in the first place, and the only one left who even cared. Nick knew that, at any moment, the crew was going to split up, and one of the boats was going to hightail it out of the swamp. He had only one card left to play, and he laid it on the table.

"I think I might know where that thing is," said Nick.

"You do?" asked Joe. "Where's dat?"

"Any of y'all know anything about an old abandoned plantation that's supposed be out here?"

"*Cho! Co!*" said Henry. "Now who's telling old children's stories?"

"We all heard dem stories since we was kids," Kirk said. "Some old, haunted plantation swallowed up by da swamp dat's home to da ghosts dat roam da night. I stopped believin' in dat 'bout da time I stopped believing in *Papa Noel*."

"Ain't no such place, Detective," agreed Joe. "I've been running 'round dese swamps my whole life and ain't never once come across it. Just ghost stories to scare the young'uns."

"Maybe, maybe not," said Nick. "You'd never seen *Bayou Noir* until yesterday neither, and never come across a creature

CLAYTON E. SPRIGGS

like the one that killed Frank, until now.'"

"I heard of it, too," Cap'n Guidry said, "and not just from children's stories. I ain't never seen it, but I heard it was real. S'posed to be out here somewheres, hidden well where no one can find it."

"It's real, alright," Dennis said at last. "I seen it."

"*Dit mon la verité*, tell da truth!" laughed Joe. "You seen it? Quite da *raconteur*, eh *Skinny Mullet*?"

"*Pic kee toi*!" Dennis spat back. "I been dere. 'Twas a long time ago. I was just a kid back den, but I ain't never forgot."

"*Coo-wee*! What a load of *merdé*," Henry said.

"*Tuat t'en grosse bueche*," Cap'n Guidry said sternly. "Let him tell us what he knows already."

"It's way deep out here," Dennis said. "Not sure exactly if we gonna be able to find it no how. It's covered by da swamp, just like dat St. Pierre place was. Have to be right up on it to know it's dere. Anyhow, I was just a kid, like I said. Come out here with my *parran*, Charlie Broussard, and one of his buddies. Any of y'all know a Louis Couvillon?"

"Didn't know him, but knew of him," Kirk said. "Some old gator hunter *coonass* from back in da day."

"I knew him," Guidry said. "Old man,

BILLY

motier foux with missing teeth. He died years ago, I heard. Knew da swamp well, or so dey say. Was *podnas* with Poppie St. Pierre's daddy too, if I remember correctly. Dat don't attest to his character none, d'oh."

"Dat be da one," Dennis said. "Used to be scared of him when I was little, too, but my *parran* said I was just being a *capon*. Anyway, come out here once when I was little, and we come across a little island, or so we thought. Covered with cypress and tupelo trees, even a few old oaks, all covered with moss. I remember dey had some old tombstones dat looked like rocks by da water. Place was real spooky; I almost pissed myself. Even my *parran* and dat old *coonass*, Couvillon, didn't want to hang around none. Dey told me not to tell anyone and never been back since. Had nightmares about it for a long time." Dennis thought about it for a few moments, then added, "Dey called it *Lost Bayou*. Trust me on dis, we don't wanna go dere."

"How a city boy like you heard about dis place, Detective?" asked Cap'n Guidry. "And why you t'ink we'll find dat t'ing dere?"

"Same way I knew about the St. Pierres, and the same way I knew that thing came out of that attic back at *Bayou Noir*," answered Nick. "One of those girls got away and is, or at least was, over at St.

Elizabeth's."

"The nut house?" asked Kenny.

"Unbelievable! Never in my life; *mais, jamais d'la vie*!" Kirk exclaimed. "You mean we following da footsteps of some *peeshwank* dat gone *bracque*?"

"Don't get all excited, Alleman," Cap'n said. "Crazy or not, dat girl been right 'bout every t'ing so far. You t'ink dat t'ing hiding over by dat old plantation, Detective?"

"Yeah, I do," said Nick. "We find that plantation; we find that creature, whatever it is."

"Whatever it be, it gonna be dead soon," Cap'n said before announcing to the group, "We goin' to *Lost Bayou*."

Chapter Twenty-Four

Two Monsters

The crew meandered through the narrow waterways amongst the overgrown cypress trees for most of the afternoon without a trace of the monster or a sign of the abandoned plantation. When pressed, Dennis would give half-hearted directions that seemed to go nowhere. He tried to tell the Cap'n over and over that he was just a small boy when he saw the island and hadn't been anywhere near it since, but Guidry wouldn't give up. As the day wore on, the thought of spending another night in the swamp weighed heavily on the group. Grumblings were beginning to be heard under the breaths of the Swamp Rats.

The boats slowed down as they passed

down a quiet *bayou*, and Nick sensed that a mutiny was about to occur. The other boat started to lag behind a bit, and Cap'n Guidry had to slow down so as not to lose sight of half of his crew. He stopped the boat and waited while Kenny kept an eye on the horizon in front of them and Nick turned to watch the others as they tried to catch up. Suddenly, he heard a scream, and the other boat rocked violently back and forth before capsizing in the shallow water. Cap'n Guidry revved up the motor and turned the boat around, racing to where the others were to aid in their rescue.

Within minutes, they came upon the other boat, but, by this time, the skiff was righted and Henry and Joseph were onboard, pulling Kirk and Dennis back in as quickly as they could.

"*Ga-lee*! What da hell happened?" asked Cap'n Guidry.

"I don't know," shouted Henry. "Kirk knocked the boat over!"

Kirk was screaming and writhing in agony and clutching at his right leg.

"*Oo ye yi*! Goddamned snake!" he screamed.

"Snake?" Kenny asked, "How'd a snake get in the boat?"

The men in the boat scrambled, searching their surroundings for another snake that

BILLY

might be hidden.

No others were in sight, and Henry prematurely announced, "It must've fell out in the water when the boat overturned."

"*Cho! Co!*" shouted Joe. "Dere's another one!"

A water moccasin slithered out from under one of the crew's wet pack that was tied to a crossbeam and hissed at the men. Henry grabbed one of the paddles and violently crushed the serpent's head with a single blow. Seconds later, another emerged from behind the supplies near the front.

"*Pic kee moi!*" shouted Dennis as he fell backwards to avoid the poisonous creature.

The snake ignored the men and slithered over the side of the boat, disappearing into the murky water. The crew poked and prodded at the remaining packs in a near panic, trying to ferret out any remaining snakes. After a few minutes, they were satisfied that none remained.

"*Coo-wee!* Y'all be careful. Don't wanna capsize again," Kenny shouted.

"*Beck moi tchew!*" replied Dennis. "I know we don't wanna capsize again, *couyon!*"

"*Ca viens?*" asked Guidry. "Is Kirk alright?"

Dennis and Joe tended to Kirk, examining his wound and trying to calm him down without much success. Finally, Joe looked up and gravely shook his head.

"*Fils de pute*! Dis can't be happenin'," Cap'n Guidry said.

"We gonna have to get him to da doctor," said Joe.

"Ain't no doctor around here," Kenny stated.

"Don't matter; we gotta try," answered Joe. "He's not gonna make it if we don't."

"Guess we better head in den," said Dennis.

"*Co faire?*" said Cap'n Guidry. "Why? I ain't goin' 'till I find dat t'ing dat killed my boy. Some of y'all take dat boat and do da best you can, but we goin' on. Dennis, you comin' wid us."

"Like hell I am," Dennis said. "I had enough. If you wanna die so bad, you do it alone. I'm goin' home."

"No, you ain't," Guidry said, lowering his shotgun and aiming it dead center at the man's chest. "You da only one here dat seen dat plantation, and we need you to find it. You comin' wid us, or I'll send you to hell right now."

Henry and Joe aimed their guns back at the obstinate old man. The tension rose quickly; no one said a word except for Kirk, who was cursing under his breath and moaning in agony.

"Let's just hold on a second, gentlemen,"

BILLY

Nick calmly stated. "Looks like we have a Mexican standoff here. We need to be reasonable and work together, or none of us will be leaving this swamp alive. Do I need to remind any of you we have more bags that need filling?"

The Swamp Rats tried to ignore him, but they also knew they weren't getting anywhere the way things were going.

Nick let them stew for a few minutes before continuing, "It's clear that one of the boats needs to get Kirk back to civilization as soon as possible. It's also clear that one of the boats is going after the beast. I'm staying with Cap'n, and Kirk is going back. It's time for the rest of y'all to decide what y'all are going to do."

"I'm going back with Kirk," said Henry.

"So am I," said Dennis.

"No, you ain't," Guidry said.

"Yes, I am," Dennis said, "and I'd advise da rest of you to do da same. Ta hell with dis old fool."

"You pushing me, *capon*," Guidry said.

"Hold on dere, now," said Joe. "You two need to calm da fuck down. Dennis, da man is right. You need to go with dem. You said yourself you been to dat place, and you da only one dat can help dem find it. If you didn't wanna go, you should've kept your mouth shut. Time to man up and do what's right. Do it for Frank; do it for Kirk."

"Kirk?" said Dennis. "He got snake bit. Ain't got nothin' to do with dat t'ing out dere."

"No?" asked Joe. "And just how you think all dem moccasins got in da boat? Don't you find dat just a tiny bit odd?"

"What you mean?" Dennis asked.

"Yeah, what you going on about, Batiste?" asked Henry.

"Dem snakes didn't jump in da boat. We all know dat can't happen," said Joe. "No, dey got t'rown in dere by somet'ing hidin' in one of dose trees over dere."

The men looked back toward the tree limbs hanging over the *bayou* behind them. Nothing could be seen, though the very real possibility that something was lurking behind the thick cover of leaves and moss made them shudder.

"And just who do you t'ink would've done dat?" continued Joe. "Our little friend, dat's who. Now, we gonna split up. Half gonna go one way, half another. Fifty-fifty which boat dat t'ing comes after. Guns or not, my money's on dat t'ing at this point. Dennis, you no safer in one boat den da other. In da end, you gotta make a choice; you gotta make da right choice. You know what I'm telling you, LeFleur?"

Dennis remained silent. He could see what

BILLY

the man was getting at, but didn't like it all the same.

"You do what's right for Frank," Nick said. "What's right for Kirk. Mostly, you do what's right for you. True, you go back, you just might make it. Might. But then what? You have to live with your decision every day after that. You remember that family back at *Bayou Noir*? Think about why they didn't go up in that attic. Fear. Fear and shame. Think about why that thing was up there in the first place. Fear and shame. You get back home, maybe you'll no longer be afraid, but the shame will cling to you forever. You want that, LeFleur? You think you can live like that? The choice is yours."

"Cap'n, put down that shotgun. Joseph, you, too. It's time for the man to make his own decision, like a man should. It's time we all respected that decision, like men should. It's time we stopped acting like a bunch of whining children and got back to the business at hand. Y'all be quick about it, or Kirk's a goner. Same for the rest of us."

Silence enveloped the group as the men looked inward and thought about the words the detective had spoken. The college boy laid it all out, the real monsters were lurking inside of each of them, fear and shame. Guidry dropped the shotgun to his side and sat back down, staring at the bag at his feet that held his only child. Henry positioned himself next to the motor on the second boat, preparing to cast off in the hopes that they could reach help in enough time to save Kirk's life. Joseph Batiste put his rifle down and sat at Kirk's side, cradling the dying man's head gently in his lap. Kenny took up position at the helm of Guidry's boat, waiting to return to the search. Lastly, Dennis dropped his rifle, reached down for his pack and threw it in the boat with the Cap'n, Nick, and Kenny. Nick holstered his weapon, reached out and grabbed Dennis's arm and helped him over.

"Welcome aboard, Dennis LeFleur," Nick said.

"Y'all get settled in," Cap'n Guidry said as he fired the engine up and the propeller came to life. "Next stop, *Lost Bayou Plantation*."

Chapter Twenty-Five

Freesons

Henry Trahan started the motor of the small boat and headed back toward civilization. He carefully avoided the overgrown branches overhead when they passed the spot where the snakes had appeared, and then increased their speed until they were cruising as fast as safely possible down the narrow waterways. Joseph sat up front, keeping his watchful eyes on the path ahead for any impediments or signs of the beast. Kirk was mostly silent now, his once-tan complexion now a ghostly white as he mumbled incoherently and foamed at the mouth while gazing a thousand yards into the unknown.

Joe turned around to look at the poor man and then glanced at Henry. No words needed to be spoken; both men understood that Kirk Alleman was going to die. Henry turned the throttle until the boat was going at maximum speed, and Joseph turned back around to help guide them safely past the overgrown swamp grass and moss-covered cypress trees up ahead.

The way out of the swamp wasn't easy. The small *bayous* they travelled down twisted and turned, and their way was frequently blocked by hyacinths or downed trees. Sometimes, the waterways would just stop, running into a patch of soggy mud or beaver damns. On more than one occasion, they had to backtrack and seek alternative ways to get out of the swamp. Time was running out for Kirk, and as the afternoon wore on, the reality of spending another night in the darkness of the Atchafalaya seemed inevitable.

"I t'ink we been dis way before," Joe said, "maybe even twice already; hard to tell. To be honest, I'm not sure if we goin' da right way or not."

"I know," Henry said, "but I t'ink I got it now. The way we come out here was blocked and when we bypassed the lilies, we got turned around. This time I'm sure I know how to go. I ain't stayin' out here past dark this time, at least not this far out here. Gonna try to get us closer in 'fore night

BILLY

comes. Hopefully give us some distance from that t'ing out there."

"By all means," said Joe. "I ain't gonna argue with dat."

By early evening, Kirk's breathing became labored, and he looked to be having intermittent seizures as his body fought hard against the toxic venom coursing through his veins. At last, Henry felt that he knew where they were, and he drove the boat as fast as he could down a narrow river, trying to get to a patch of open water he believed to be ahead of them before night fell.

"*Ga-lee!*" shouted Joseph. "You need to slow down. Dere's trees everywhere, and worse yet, dere's a gator pond just up ahead. We don't wanna hit one of dem branches and fall in da water 'round here, not when we already come dis far."

Henry ignored the man. He thought he now knew where they were and where they were going. He knew Batiste was right; there was an infamous gator hole they were coming up on, and anyone who fell in the water was going to be dinner for the hungry reptiles. The gators were already well on their way to waking up and preparing for their nocturnal hunt for food. He didn't want to be stuck out there past sundown, even on the boat.

Joe could see the open area up ahead just

beyond a patch of ground overgrown with bushes and moss-covered trees. One more swift turn to the right and they were home free. Henry stood up in the back, one hand clutching the rudder, the wind in his face. He began to smile at the welcome sight up ahead and turned the throttle even more in anticipation of escaping the dense confines of the swampland behind them. His face beamed with relief as they skirted past the oak and cypress trees and hungry alligators at the final turn and on toward the open water up ahead.

Henry spotted an unexpected movement from the bark on the tree to his right, but before he could react in time, a sharp, metal hook swung around and caught him in the eye socket, jamming into his skull and turning his brain into mush. A steel cable was attached to one end of the hook and the other end was fastened around one of the cypress knots jutting up all around them. As the boat sped forward, Henry's body was brutally yanked into the murky water in an instant.

The sudden jerk caused Joe to squeeze off a useless round from his hunting rifle as the boat spun wildly. Within seconds, the vessel capsized, making Joe drop his firearm and spilling Joe and Kirk into the drink. Alligators appeared all around them, drawn

BILLY

to the helpless prey thrashing about within the grasp of their sharp teeth and powerful jaws. Three of the larger beasts tore violently at Henry's body, tearing off limbs and globs of bloody flesh in the process. Several others ascended on what was left of Kirk Alleman's weakened remains, fighting amongst themselves for the right to devoir the poor victim.

Joseph Batiste felt a sharp pain in his right foot and was suddenly jerked under the surface of the shallow water. His body began to spin violently, and his breath was knocked out by the sudden jolt, putrid swamp water filling his lungs. He instinctively panicked and yanked his mangled foot free of the hungry reptile's mouth, pushing to the surface and onto the mound of dirt nearby. Miraculously, he scrambled up a tree just in time to escape the ferocious beasts below.

Joseph held on to the branches tightly, spitting out the nasty water and trying to catch his breath. His heart was pounding, and he shivered in the damp air as he gazed down at the horrendous sight below. Dozens of hungry alligators tore at what was left of his friends, and occasionally fighting amongst themselves for the tasty morsels. Three or four of the hardy creatures that were left out of the feeding frenzy snapped at the foot of the tree, their soulless eyes looking directly into his, waiting for him to drop and fill their stomachs.

Joe began to cry. *Oo ye yi*, he thought, what am I going to do? The boat was lost and their guns with it. There he was, all alone and defenseless, hiding in a tree surrounded by angry gators that had nothing to do but wait for their next meal to tire and fall. He looked down again and saw that the reptiles at his feet were quiet. They just stared up at him, but were no longer making a sound. The hair on Joe's neck stood up, and he felt his heart drop into the pit of his stomach. There was something behind him in the tree.

Batiste turned around and saw the beast for the first time. The creature was almost as big as he was, with two red, beady eyes that stared straight into his, burning fear into his heart. It had a nose like a man's and was covered with dirt, moss, and bark that made it almost invisible to the naked eye against the backdrop of the dense vegetation. The thing had two arms that ended in sharp claw-like hands, two legs that were froglike, though sporting powerful muscles and webbed feet with sharp nails. Its hands and feet appeared too big, each seeming to have extra appendages not seen on any natural creature.

Joe looked at the thing in fear and disgust. He stared into the face of the beast and froze

BILLY

in horror. The thing was smiling at him, smiling at him with big, sharp teeth while a foul odor emanated out of the freakishly large mouth that encompassed the entire lower half of the monster's head. To Joseph's horror, he could see that the thing wasn't a thing at all, it was a boy.

"Eeeeeeeeaaaaaaagggggghhhhh!" it roared in triumph.

The sudden howl took Joe by surprise and his wet fingers slipped off of the damp tree limbs, sending him barreling backwards to the ground below. His body hit the thick mud and roots with a painful thud and knocked the wind out of his lungs. Before he could move, the gators were upon him. He shrieked in agony as the reptiles tore into his flesh and bones, spilling his organs into the rotting vegetation to be devoured by birds and insects once the larger predators were through.

The last thing Joseph Batiste saw before his eyes closed for good was the sight of a sad, deformed boy staring down at him from the safety of a cypress tree, laughing with malevolent delight.

CLAYTON E. SPRIGGS

Chapter Twenty-Six

Lost Bayou

After the group split up, Cap'n Guidry got back to the task at hand. He guided what was left of the crew further into the swamp. Sometimes, he would ask Dennis if he recognized anything, which the man would deny more often than not, and other times he proceeded based upon whatever gut-feelings he had. None of the others argued, since Guidry's knowledge of the swamp and ability to track its nefarious inhabitants were well known. As the afternoon progressed, it seemed to Nick that they were lost, though he kept the unpleasant thought to himself.

"*Coo-wee!*" said Guidry. "Look at dat."

They drifted up to a small patch of dry land covered with high grass and weeds and looked to where Cap'n was pointing. Barely visible in the soft earth were footprints, six toes on each. Nick was amazed that the old man saw them in the first place, and he was grateful that they were being led by such a capable guide.

"It looks like he been here recently," stated Guidry, "and looks like he was headed down dere."

Cap'n nodded toward a narrow *bayou* that ran through a heavily-wooded section of the swamp. The crew sat back and steadied their guns, half expecting the monster to jump out at them at any moment. Guidry slowly guided the boat down the dark *bayou*, hoping they would reach their destination before night fell and the ever-threatening thunderclouds overhead came to life.

"Dis looks familiar," said Dennis, his voice noticeably shaken by the revelation. "I t'ink we gettin' close."

The men were silent, watching and listening intently for any sign of the beast. To the relief of everyone, nothing out of place was in sight, and the loud singing of birds and croaking of frogs serenaded them. The crew came to realize that the swamp seemed to get quiet when the creature was lurking around, so any sounds produced by the indigenous wildlife was a welcomed sign.

"Look over there," said Kenny, pointing up

BILLY

ahead. "There's some more of those markings on the trees."

"Dat t'ing's been here, alright," said Guidry. "We on its trail."

As much as the terrible beast struck fear into the group, the men were grateful that they were able to track it. For one thing, it meant that they were not lost, but actively engaged in hunting the animal. It also gave the crew a psychological boost; they were in control. There were four of them, all heavily armed. Sure, the mysterious creature was dangerous, but so were they. Up to now, the monster had them chasing their tales. Now, they were on its heels.

"It can run, but it can't hide," said Cap'n. "We gonna find it and we gonna kill it. Its days are numbered. It's gonna pay for killin' my boy."

"I t'ink we almost dere," said Dennis. "I'm sure of it. Dis place giving me da *freesons*. I remember it from my nightmares."

"You gonna remember it again, *Skinny Mullet*," said Guidry. "Only dis time, you gonna remember it with pride."

"Look, there's some rocks," Kenny said, pointing to some grey stone outcroppings on an island up ahead.

The sun was almost down by the time they drifted up to the island. The dark clouds and moss-covered trees made it almost pitch black, even in the twilight hours, but they made it before nightfall all the same. The crew retrieved their flashlights, and Kenny tied the boat to one of the nearby rocks.

"*Cho! Co!* There's a name on this one," Kenny said. "Colette Deslautier. I can't make out the rest. These rocks are tombstones; we're in a graveyard."

"*Dit mon la verite*," whispered Dennis. "Dis be da place."

Once the boat was secured, the crew slowly scanned the horizon, looking for any sign of the beast. It began to drizzle, so the men unpacked a few needed items and headed for the relative shelter of some nearby oak trees. Once under the giant canopy of moss-covered limbs, Kenny and Nick began to make a small fire while Guidry and Dennis kept a watchful eye.

"T'ink it's a good idea to start a fire?" asked Dennis. "It'll lead dat t'ing straight to us."

"Dat t'ing already going to find us here, *couyon*," Cap'n Guidry answered. "I doubt da fire gonna make much difference. Besides, we need to dry up a bit and get some warmth. Dese batteries ain't gonna keep dese lights running all night. Dis way, we can save dem for when we need dem da most."

The crew sat around the fire, quietly

BILLY

listening to the sounds of the swamp while enjoying what little warmth the small flame provided. It was almost night time when they heard the distant sound of a gunshot.

"Hear that?" Kenny asked. "You think that was from the others?"

"Most likely," Nick answered. "I doubt if anyone else is this far out here, especially at sundown."

The men nodded in agreement. They knew that the stories of the monster kept all but the hardiest of fishermen and hunters out of the area, and even those weren't about to come this far into the swamp in the dark. The Swamp Rats were on their own to the bitter end.

"You t'ink dey got it?" Dennis asked.

A few moments passed before they heard the unwelcome roar of the beast echo through the trees. The men's hearts sank with the realization that their friends had run into the monster, and the monster had prevailed. If the creature was still alive, they all knew that chances were the other men weren't.

"*Fils de pute!*" Cap'n Guidry spat. "I swear I'm gonna rip dat t'ing to pieces when I get my hands on it."

"It sounded like it was far off," said Kenny. "Maybe we'll be safe through the night."

"Maybe," said Dennis, "but I ain't countin' on it. Dat t'ing ain't natural. It's some kind of demon. It'll be here 'fore long, and it's coming for blood."

"*Tuat t'en grosse bueche, Skinny Mullet!*" said Cap'n. "It's comin' alright, but it ain't no demon. Dat t'ing's flesh and blood, same as us. Da only blood gonna be shed is dat t'ing's blood."

Cap'n Guidry glanced toward the boat where his only son's body lay lifeless in a zippered black bag. He cradled the shotgun in his hands before he continued, "Let it come; we waitin' on it."

Chapter Twenty-Seven

Make the Misere'

Before long, night descended on the Swamp Rats. They took turns surveying the area, always going out two at a time and never traveling out of sight of the small fire that they'd built. Nick sat next to Cap'n Guidry, looking at the trees that surrounded them. He could see that the dark limbs of the massive oaks and the dense vegetation of the swamp were covering an even more ancient structure underneath. Nick remembered the words Margaret had spoken while under her trance, and he knew exactly what lay hidden in the dark.

He quietly whispered a name, "*Lost Bayou Plantation.*"

Cap'n Guidry looked at the detective for a

moment and let the distant memories of his childhood rise to the surface.

"Da House of Slaughter," he said.

Nick looked at the old man in the soft, dancing light of the campfire. Guidry's hair was wet from the drizzling rain that fell gently through the trees, and he looked ten years older than he did just days ago at the start of their mission. Their mission, thought Nick. So much for that. Even he no longer cared if they found any trace of the missing kids. He knew what happened to them. The girl in the insane asylum already told them, they just refused to believe it. She'd been right about everything. Nick believed her now.

"It's an old story dat my granddaddy passed on to me when I was young," Guidry said. "Just some old ghost stories to scare da children, keep dem from going out into da swamp alone. Haunted plantation from da old days. Supposed to be cursed, legend has it. 'Twas a cruel place to be, even by da standards of da day. Old man run it gone *bracque* when his wife died, and when he passed it on to his bastard child, da man started torturing da slaves. Some tried to run off, but dere's nowhere to go dis far out in da swamp. T'ings came to a head, and da slaves revolted. Back den, if da slaves fought back, dey would kill dem all, or worse. Story

BILLY

goes, dey kept to themselves, hoping no one would find out. No one ever came out here, so dey just tried to survive as best dey could. A flood washed away da road; deir boats sunk. T'ings got bad, but by den, dey was stuck. Dey had no way out, and most knew even if dey could make it out, dey'd be tortured and killed. So dey stayed put. When food got scarce, da stories say, dey turned on each other."

"Cannibals?" Nick asked in horror.

Cap'n Guidry nodded. "Dat's what dey say. Eventually, dey all died, but never passed on, if you know what I mean."

"Ghosts," said Nick. He had never believed in the supernatural, but he knew that, just days ago, he didn't believe in monsters, either. By now, nothing was off limits.

"Well, dat's how dem stories go anyway," Cap'n said, then added, "At least, it kept us outta da swamp."

Nick laughed. "Yeah, I guess it did."

The rain began to come down harder, and Dennis and Kenny made their way back to the others. They all hunched over near the flame, trying in vain to stay dry. Flashes of lightning and bellows of thunder occasionally erupted throughout the night, startling the wet and frightened men huddled by the fire. The hours wore on without a sign of the beast.

"If it keeps coming down like this, the boat's going to fill up and sink," said Kenny.

"Yeah, you probably right 'bout dat," Guidry replied. "Best you go have a look."

Kenny got up, leaving the relative shelter under the oak trees, and jogged out into the rain to check on the boat. A flash of lightning lit up the sky, and a blast of thunder shook the wet earth below. Minutes ticked by, but Kenny never returned.

"Kenny," shouted Cap'n. "Hurry da hell up already!"

The men waited, but no reply came. The crew grew quiet and listened intently, but all was silent except for the sound of the falling rain and occasional boom of thunder. Gone were the sounds of croaking frogs and chirping crickets. The men glanced at each other, then back to where Kenny disappeared into the rain. Nick sighed with relief when the shadowy figure of their friend emerged from the darkness and headed toward them. A flash of lightning lit up the sky, temporarily illuminating the figure coming their way. The men looked on in horror. The approaching figure wasn't Kenny.

"*Pic kee moi*!" shouted Dennis. "What da fuck?"

The men sprung to their feet and fired into the darkness. When the gunfire abated,

BILLY

they peered into the night, praying they would spot the lifeless body of the slain beast before them. Nick grabbed his flashlight and pointed it in the direction from which the figure had emerged. There was nothing there.

"*Merde*!" Guidry said. "Not a goddamned t'ing."

"*Que c'est q 'ca*?" shouted Dennis.

The dead leaves and grass around them suddenly came alive with the sound of something coming up fast from their left. The men turned and fired. Seconds later a round object rolled toward them, stopping at their feet.

"Motherfucker!" shouted Nick.

Cap'n Guidry felt his stomach retch as he stared down at Kenneth Nunez's decapitated head, its empty eye sockets dripping blood and brain matter and its mouth grinning wildly.

"*Oo ye yi*!" Dennis said. "*Pic kee toi feet pue tan*! Fuck you, you goddamned son of a bitch!"

Panicked with terror, Dennis ran out into the rain and fired randomly into the surrounding bush. Nick instinctively dropped to the ground and steadied his firearm. He heard a horrendous shriek and saw Guidry fall to the earth.

"Aaaaaaggh! *Co faire*?," Cap'n shouted.

"You done shot me, you goddamned *Skinny Mullet*!"

Nick crawled to where the old man lay. There was blood oozing from the right side of Guidry's abdomen, and he held his side and moaned. Nick swung around toward Dennis, who was standing in the rain, looking at the damage he had caused.

"I'm sorry!" he yelled. "I'm so sorry, Cap'n. I didn't mean it. It was an accident!"

Nick watched in horror as a figure appeared behind Dennis. He aimed his pistol, but was unable to get a clear shot without endangering the man. Nick shouted a warning to Dennis, but it was drowned out by a sudden crash of thunder.

"Dennis, look out!"

"I'm sorry," shouted Dennis again. "I swear it was an accident!"

"Dennis!" Nick yelled again. "Behind you!"

It was too late. Just as Dennis turned around, the monster was close behind him. Without hesitation, the beast swung his powerful arm at the man's midsection, ripping a portion of his intestines out and spilling blood and internal organs onto the ground. With his other arm, the creature grabbed hold of Dennis' wrist, causing his gun to fall uselessly away; then he ripped the man's arm completely out of its socket. Dennis screamed in shock and agony, but his

BILLY

pleas were quickly cut off when the beast opened its monstrous jaws and bit the man's face with its sharp, jagged teeth.

Nick pointed his gun toward the pair and unloaded his clip. When his gun was empty, there was nothing in sight but the bloody remains of Dennis LeFleur, torn to pieces on the wet earth, steam radiating off the warm flesh. Nick scanned the horizon, straining his eyes to see through the darkness and rain. He quickly reached into his jacket pocket, tearing open a waterproof bag and replacing the empty clip in his Glock. Looking around again, he saw no sign of the creature. Nick knew it was here somewhere, and it was going to come back for him. He scrambled back to Guidry's side.

"Cap'n," he whispered, "you still here?"

"Yeah," groaned the injured man. "You bet your sweet ass I am. You see what dat t'ing did to LeFleur? *Fils de pute*! I ain't never seen no t'ing like dat in my life."

"Me neither, Cap'n," Nick replied. "Me neither."

"Da whole time I be t'inking we trackin' it, but it be settin' its trap. You listen to me, Detective. Dis t'ing ain't no ordinary animal; it's clever. It outsmarted all of us."

Guidry grunted and clenched his teeth from the pain in his side, shifting his weight before continuing, "Now, it be well known dat da most dangerous animal to hunt is a wounded animal, 'specially when it's cornered. Right now, dat be me. I ain't gonna make it out of here no how, but I ain't lettin' dat t'ing take me out neither. Here, take my shotgun."

Guidry handed Nick the only thing he had left in this world. "Now, you give me dat pistol. Dat t'ing gonna come back soon to finish us off. I'll make some noise to distract it while you sneak over dere by dem rocks. Soon as dat t'ing makes its move, I'm gonna keep it busy. You run, and keep running. Don't hesitate, and don't turn around. Just keep goin'."

"But you saw what that thing did to Dennis," Nick pleaded. "There's no way I'm going to leave you out here to die alone."

"I'm a goner anyway. Dat dumbass *Skinny Mullet* done shot me t'rough da liver. I ain't got long. You just keep goin'. I'm gonna get dat t'ing, and I'm gonna get him good."

"I can't do that, Cap'n" said Nick.

"Can't? *Pic kee toi*! Do as I say!" Guidry replied. "Don't you worry 'bout me, Nicholas Vizier. I'll keep one of dem bullets for myself, just in case."

"Just in case," Nick repeated, and the two men looked at each other and smiled, remembering the requested body bags before their smiles faded with the thought of Frank,

BILLY

Jr.'s mangled corpse filling the first one.

"You go on now, Vizier," said Guidry. "Dere's not much time left. You make it out of here, and don't ever look back. Dat t'ing come from hell, and I'm sending it back tonight."

Nick nodded. There was nothing left for him to say. He took Cap'n's shotgun and crawled through the rain and mud until he got to the ancient tombstones that stood watch over the haunted island of Lost Bayou Plantation. Nick looked back toward the giant oak trees in time to see a blast of lightning flash across the sky. In the temporary radiance, the outline of the forlorn plantation house was clearly visible. The House of Slaughter, thought Nick; the name fit. Cap'n Guidry's last words echoed in his head: "Send that t'ing back to hell". It'll be a short trip, he thought. It's already there.

Nick crouched silently amongst the tombstones and waited, keeping as quiet and still as he could, trying to fade into the shadows.

"Eeeeeeeeeaaaaaaaaggggghhh!" the beast roared from a hidden spot near where Guidry lie.

Nick heard gunshots and ran into the darkness of the swamp. Just as Cap'n Guidry instructed, he never looked back and never returned to that haunted place again.

CLAYTON E. SPRIGGS

Chapter Twenty-Eight

Mal Pris

Nicholas ran as fast as he could manage through the dense vegetation. When the water got deep, he swam. He knew that he was surrounded by vicious and unseen predators that haunted the swamp in the night, but instinct kept him moving forward. Nick was no longer scared of the alligators and snakes all around him. He was running away from something much worse.

He'd been traveling for only a short time when he heard the gunshots erupt from behind him. Nick climbed up on a small outcropping of land in order to catch his breath, and listened. Loud, staccato bursts from his Glock rang out in the night, followed by another round of four or five shots. Minutes later, he heard one more shot before the eerie silence returned. Nick waited to hear the dreadful roar of the victorious beast, but no further sound was heard. He sighed with relief when the croaking of frogs and chirping of crickets returned.

Nicholas thought about heading back toward Lost Bayou Plantation, but he remembered the words that Cap'n Guidry had spoken. That thing was smart. Nick thought that it could be a trap. The beast could be keeping quiet in order to lure him out of hiding only to devour him when he returned. It didn't matter, thought Nick. He had promised Guidry that he was going to get out of there and not look back, no matter what. That's just what he intended to do.

Nick was forced to slow down as he tried to navigate his way through the swamp at night. After an hour or so, he climbed into a big oak tree to wait for daylight to return. He listened intently to the sounds of the insects and creatures around him, but heard none that alerted him to the return of the beast. He knew by now that the other denizens of the hostile environment held their own breaths when the monster was around, so as long as Nick could hear the other animals lurking about, he was reasonably assured that the terrifying creature was not around.

BILLY

The detective sat alone in the tree and peered into the darkness all around him. The air was thick, and a fine mist floated over the stagnant water, giving off an eerie, green glow in small areas. Nick remembered, when he was a child, his mother used to tell him stories about the luminous patches of fog, that they were really ghostly apparitions from beyond the grave, the forsaken spirits damned to roam the bogs for eternity. He knew that, in reality, it was just methane gas rising from the multitude of rotting vegetation that the swamp produced. After what he'd just experienced, Nick wondered if his dear, departed mother's explanation was closer to the truth.

A sudden rustle of leaves to his left interrupted Nick's thoughts. He froze in fear as he realized there was something in the tree with him. Nick held his breath and pulled the shotgun closer to his side. An unexpected sound almost made him slip and fall into the darkness below.

"Whoooo!"

Nick laughed. "A fucking owl," he muttered underneath his breath in relief. The detective was grateful for the company. He figured that as long as the bird of prey was next to him, the beast wasn't. Of course, the owl could just fly away at the first inkling of danger, thought Nick. But the fact that he remained was a promising sign that Nick was safe, at least for the moment. Nicholas couldn't see shit in the dark, but the feathered nocturnal predator could see all.

Nick thought about the events that brought him to this desolate place. He thought of how he had abandoned his loving mother to fend for herself all those years ago. He remembered that he had always intended to go back and rescue her once he was successful enough. Life taught him too late that the definition of 'enough' was a moving target that most people could never attain. In the end, he made a life for himself over in New Orleans, while his mother waited for a day that never came. Nick felt shame and guilt for what he had done, for what he had failed to do, and there was nothing he could ever do now to redeem himself for his sin. His mother was gone; her son had never returned.

The rational side of Nick told him that it ended up being for the best. The area in which his home had been, in eastern New Orleans, quickly deteriorated not long after he moved there. Violent crime was rampant. Nick worked long hours, and his poor Evangeline would have been all alone in an unfamiliar and hostile environment. It would've been a scary place for an old Cajun

BILLY

country girl to spend her last days. In the end, Hurricane Katrina washed it all away while Nick was out of town. Evangeline Vizier would have met the same fate that the St. Pierres had met. No, she had been better off without him – a sentiment that did little to comfort Nick's tortured soul.

He thought about Marie Leblanc, about how he'd left without a word when the only girl he'd ever loved ran off with the ignorant and cruel Ronald Savoy. Nick always told himself that she was probably better off anyway. Ronnie's family had money. He could give her a life that Nick never could. Those illusions had been shattered upon his return. Marie suffered greatly for her mistake, a mistake that might not have happened if Nick would only have put up more of a fight to keep her all those years ago. In the end, he had just left, abandoning her as he had his mother.

Now, he had returned. Nick had come rolling back into town after all those years; not as a conquering hero, but as a failure who'd been all but run out of town, his town. The detective had run out on the historic and glorious city of New Orleans that had given Nick a sense of purpose, a home, a career. He'd been high and dry in the Rocky Mountains learning the latest techniques to aid him in the successful searches for missing persons. All the good that did him now, with him sitting in a tree, lost in the swamp, and hiding from some kind of unholy creature that was out for blood, his blood, Nick thought.

He knew it was unlikely that he would get out alive. Just as well, he figured. It was what he deserved. Nick had brought those brave men out into the swamp to find a group of lost college kids, and he had gotten everyone killed. There was no sign of the lost search party, and the detective knew now that there never would be. The Swamp Rats had all been murdered, torn limb from limb, by a beast everyone had warned him about. What would await Nick even if he did manage to find his way out of the Atchafalaya Basin alive? There would be only questions he could not answer, accusations he could not refute, and the look of disappointment in the eyes of the only woman he had ever loved.

After what seemed an eternity, dawn finally arrived. A thick fog enveloped the area, but Nick knew that it wouldn't be long before the intense heat of the southern sun burnt it away. He carefully climbed out of the stately oak tree and relieved himself at its base. He stretched out his aching back and sore limbs, rechecked his meager supplies and Guidry's shotgun, and then

BILLY

picked a direction in which to proceed. Nick no longer knew with any certainty which way to go. He had no boat and no compass, and even if he had, he had no earthly idea of where he was in the first place. His gut told him that Lost Bayou and The House of Slaughter were behind him, and that made choosing his way easy. He started off in the opposite direction.

Nick struggled to make his way through the rough terrain. Over and over again, he found his path impassable, and he had to find an alternative route in order to go anywhere. He spotted the same locations that he'd previously passed hours before on more than one occasion. As the day wore on and evening approached, Nick harbored no illusions – he was hopelessly lost. Just before sunset, he found a dry patch of dirt and built a small fire, then settled down for the night. He was terrified that the beast would see the flame and descend upon his campsite while he slept, so he tried to keep a sharp eye out for as long as he could. It had been days since he'd slept and, in the end, his fatigue won the battle against his fear, and he drifted off to sleep.

Nick's eyes sprung open, and he sat up abruptly. His fire was out and the sun was almost directly overhead. He had survived another night. Nick rebuilt the fire and filled his canteen with the brackish water that surrounded him. He filtered it as best he could through the cloth of his filthy shirt, then let it boil awhile over the small flame as he prepared to move on for another day. His stomach cramped with hunger, and he searched all around him for something to fill it. The best he could find was a couple of crawfish, and he scooped them up and heated them for a moment on the fire before devouring them. Nick never remembered anything tasting so good in his entire life, and he unsuccessfully searched the area for more. Once his canteen had cooled enough for him to carry, Nick set out once again in search of civilization.

Another night came, then another. As hard as Nick tried to find food and maintain enough clean drinking water, he knew he couldn't keep it up. He was becoming dehydrated in the hot, humid climate, and the exertion from his forays through the dense overgrowth sapped him of any strength that the small morsels he could find to eat provided him. Mosquitoes, fire ants, and chiggers had torn into his flesh so much that he felt like one giant blister. Only one week had passed since he and the men had set out on their ill-fated quest, and Nick knew he wouldn't last another week. He was slowly dying. If the beast didn't kill him, the swamp surely would.

"*Mal pris*, as you used to say, Mama," Nick whispered to himself. "I'm stuck in a bad way."

CLAYTON E. SPRIGGS

Chapter Twenty-Nine

The Way Home

Nicholas lost count of the days as he wandered through the swamp. He felt his body start to go and his mind with it. His skin was covered with scratches and mosquito bites, and his feet burned from some sort of fungus that had taken root in his damp socks and wet boots. His tongue felt like a dry sponge, devoid of moisture, yet it continuously ran across his chapped lips in a useless effort to add comfort to his parched, cracked skin.

He told himself that he no longer cared if he lived or died. He tried to convince himself that if the beast were to suddenly appear before him, he would welcome the release of death, preferring to end it all rather than to go on suffering this way. But, he knew that was a lie every time he pushed past the next obstacle in his way, or clutched the shotgun tightly when he got spooked. Nick wanted to live; let the chips fall where they may.

By the following afternoon, he spotted an old cabin in the distance. He swam across a shallow pond until he found a stretch of soggy mud that led toward the back of the abandoned dwelling. Random debris lie scattered about the area, some of which he realized he could use to aid in his survival.

It was clear that the house itself hadn't been in use for some time, though it looked vaguely familiar to the detective. He felt a knot in the pit of his stomach, and he froze on the spot. He knew where he was. The words Cap'n Guidry spoke a lifetime ago echoed in his head: "On behalf of Cap'n Guidry and the Swamp Rats, I welcome you to *Bayou Noir*."

He slowly and quietly approached the small cabin from the rear, looking for any sign of movement. There was none. He crept down the wooden pier and around the front, staying as far away from the dilapidated structure as he could. Nick spotted a small pirogue off to the side and carried it to an open area by the dock out front. He paused and surveyed his surroundings. Nothing stirred. Nick glanced back toward the house

BILLY

and the cryptic message painted in red near the front doorway. 4 DB, WA indeed, thought Nick.

Off to the side, the detective spotted a small trolling motor and a can of gasoline. He ran past the house and retrieved the much needed items, then secured the motor to the aft of the small boat. He searched the area again, this time he managed to find an empty plastic container and some random fishing gear that he was sure he could use if he got stuck on his way in.

The birds were singing, the cicadas chirping loudly in the trees, and Nick even heard the occasional fish jumping in the water. A few clouds drifted past the sun overhead, giving him some temporary relief from the intense sunlight that scorched his exposed skin. A cool breeze blew across the quiet water, and it began to drizzle. Nick looked to the heavens and closed his eyes, enjoying the sensation of being alive.

He took a deep breath and got back to work, securing the last of his meager supplies and preparing to cast off, when he stopped in his tracks. He felt the hair on the back of his neck stand up, and he turned abruptly, looking over his shoulder at the small cabin at his back. He could see nothing in the darkness of the shack beyond the open space where the front door once stood, but

Nick knew there was something there. The birds were no longer singing, the insects were quiet, and not a sound could be heard in that godforsaken place save for the falling rain.

He turned back around and reached over to start the motor. His hand held on to the throttle for a moment, then he removed it. He reached down and snatched Cap'n Guidry's shotgun, then turned back toward the house and got out of the boat. He took a deep breath and steadied himself. He walked toward the open cabin doorway to meet his fate.

As he neared the small opening, Nick noticed the unmistakable blood trail that led into the house. Guidry got the damn thing after all, thought Nick. Good for him. The detective knew that even if Cap'n had wounded it, he hadn't killed it. The trail led here, which meant Cap'n Francois Guidry met his maker at the hands of the monster, giving rise to yet another restless spirit to haunt the forgotten graveyard of Lost Bayou Plantation. There was one more soul destined to join them, thought Nick, as he raised the shotgun in his hands and entered the house.

Once inside, he paused to allow his eyes to adjust to the darkness and listened intently to the quiet that surrounded him. Fading in

BILLY

and out, Nick could hear the barely audible sounds of labored breathing. It came from the small space above. The detective's eyes followed the fresh droplets of blood on the wooden ladder into the dark, square hole that led into the attic. Every fiber in his being told him to turn around and run, to forget the terrible things he had witnessed, and get in the boat and sail away, never to return. He stood at the bottom rung of the ladder and froze, not knowing what to do.

He thought about the speech he'd given to Dennis LeFleur in order to persuade him to carry on with the search. He thought of the two monsters that existed within every man, the two that would be scratching at the door of a man's soul forever, struggling to manipulate his actions for their own sadistic pleasure. The two monsters ruled the St. Pierre household, forcing them to create a beast that sealed their own fates and unleashing an unrelenting terror into the world. In his mind, he spoke the names of the two monsters, while aloud, he spoke the only two words his mouth could form.

"Fuck it."

Nick held the shotgun tightly in his right hand and climbed up the ladder.

CLAYTON E. SPRIGGS

Chapter Thirty

Monster

When he got to the top of the ladder, Nick paused for a moment to steady himself, then he poked his head through the small opening. A hole torn into the rusted, tin roof allowed enough sunlight to come in for the detective to see into the hot, confined space. The area behind him was empty save for a few pieces of old furniture covered with cobwebs. At the other end, just past Poppie St. Pierre's rotting corpse, a fresh trail of blood led to some kind of animal hidden in the shadows. Whatever it was, it was injured. Nick remembered Cap'n Guidry's warning about the dangers of cornering a wounded animal, but he'd come too far to turn back now. He climbed up into the attic.

Once Nick got his footing, he carefully stepped around the foul carcass at his feet and leveled the shotgun. The creature was lying in a pool of blood, intermittently breathing hard and fast at times, and almost not breathing at other times. Nick knew that this was a sign that it was close to death. Close or not, he thought, I'm going to send it the rest of the way.

The thing ignored his presence, seemingly unaware that the armed man was standing before him, pointing a shotgun in his direction. As Nick's eyes acclimated to the light, he scanned the area around the beast in morbid curiosity.

Fastened to a wooden post, lay a pile of rusty chains that had once kept the monster at bay, and Nick could make out markings scratched into the rotting cypress floor, apparently made by the beast during his torturous captivity. He turned his gaze back to the dying animal and saw that it held something in its hands.

The beast's left hand was hidden from sight, but, in his right hand, Nick clearly recognized the unwelcome item. The detective felt a cold wave of fear sweep over his body; the beast was holding his Glock.

Guidry's shotgun had not left Nick's grasp for days, and he finally put it to use. He felt his hands tighten around the firearm, and he

BILLY

pulled the trigger. A small, feeble click echoed off the walls of the small chamber. The detective felt a wave of panic and pulled back again – nothing.

He looked over at his intended target; his panic reached an overwhelming level when he saw the beast's beady, red eyes staring back into his own. Nick looked down at his own gun cradled in the monster's claw, and his heart dropped when the thing followed his gaze. He couldn't be sure, but he almost detected a small laugh come from the beast at the irony of it all. It didn't really matter now, Nick thought, he was toast.

The creature pointed the Glock at Nick and watched the detective's reaction. Nicholas Vizier never felt so helpless in his life. After everything, it had come down to this. His arms fell to his sides, and he let Guidry's useless shotgun fall to the floor. Then he met the monster's gaze.

"Go on," said Nick. "Do it."

The beast cocked his head to the side and looked at him in silence.

"What are you waiting for?" Nick asked. "Go ahead and kill me. I deserve it."

The creature was unmoved. It stared back at him, seemingly waiting for the detective to continue his pleas.

"You might as well," Nick continued. "There's no one going to miss me; no one waiting for my return. I'm sure you'd know all about that, whatever you are."

The creature aimed the gun at Nick's chest; Nick shut his eyes and held his breath in anticipation. Nothing happened. He looked again at the beast, only to see the creature put the gun on the dusty floor in front of him. The thing gazed up at Nick, then kicked the handgun across the floorboards to come to rest at the detective's feet. He quickly reached down and picked up his lost firearm, then promptly inspected the gun this time to see if it was loaded. To his surprise, it was. He exhaled with elation at his sudden good fortune and aimed the gun at the beast.

The thing was no longer looking at him. It was breathing hard again, seemingly preoccupied with the hidden object in its other claw. Terrified that the thing would produce yet another weapon, Nick pointed his gun toward the beast and took a couple of steps forward.

The thing ignored the detective completely. The strange behavior and reaction, or non-reaction, that the creature displayed caused Nick to hesitate. He had witnessed with his own eyes the ferociousness of the beast. He had looked on helplessly as it tore his friends' bodies apart, limb from limb. Something here didn't quite

BILLY

fit.

Nick peered into the shadows and struggled to see what the creature was doing. His eyes suddenly saw several markings scratched into the wooden floorboards around the creature, and he was shocked as one set of symbols came into focus. As he deciphered the crudely written word at the monster's feet, Nick's mouth opened, and he unconsciously spoke the word aloud.

"Billy?"

The creature's labored panting briefly stopped, and it turned and looked at the detective.

Nick looked back into the beast's eyes and repeated the name he had just spoken, "Billy."

To his horror, the beast smiled at him.

The gun in his hand suddenly exploded, interrupting the eerie silence of the small attic. Nick's ears rang from the loud and unexpected noise, and the muscles of his arm ached from the abrupt kickback. The unmistakable smell of gunpowder filled the confined space, and he felt a wave of nausea rise from his belly. He looked over at the creature and saw that it was no longer breathing. Nicholas Vizier had killed the beast.

The detective walked closer to the

unmoving creature at his feet and saw the object that it had held in its deformed hand. It was a faded picture of a pretty, young Cajun girl with an engaging, crooked smile and a sad, faraway look in her big, round eyes. Lillian St. Pierre, thought Nick, Billy's mother. The detective fell to his knees and began to weep.

He thought about all of the things that had led him to this event, all of the people he had lost along the way. He thought about his imminent return, of finally becoming the conquering hero he had always wanted to be. Nicholas Vizier, the man that overcame the fear of certain death and killed the terrifying monster that haunted the Atchafalaya Swamp.

He imagined the fanfare upon his return. The proud look in Marie's loving eyes as the legend of the brave detective spread throughout the region, maybe even the country. Images swam in his head of countless interviews and rounds of applause that would meet him as he toured the world, regaling his adoring audiences with his great adventures. His smiling picture on the cover of prominent magazines, some even with him posing next to the terrifying monster that he had slain.

He felt disgusted; he felt dirty. He may have overcome his fear when he climbed up

BILLY

into that attic, but the other monster rejoiced with victory. No matter what anyone could ever claim, he knew he was no slayer of demons. No, it was more like he murdered a helpless and dying animal. He knew even this wasn't the truth. He knew it was no animal that lay murdered at his feet, it was a boy. Nick had murdered a defenseless child.

And what of that child, thought Nick. Born out of sin, abused out of shame, and tortured out of fear, the sad, deformed child only became what others had forced him to become. Scorn and ridicule had been the only things that his fellow human beings had ever shared with him. He wasn't a monster, nor a beast; not a creature, nor a demon; and he never had been. His name was Billy, and he had been a person. If Nick were to return the conquering hero, there was only one role Billy had left to play – the sad role he had been tortured with his entire life. Nick knew what he had to do.

CLAYTON E. SPRIGGS

Chapter Thirty-One

Hero

Nick sailed away that afternoon from *Bayou Noir*, only turning around once to glance passed his shoulder and get one last look at the final resting place of the St. Pierre family. By now, the tall column of black smoke reached the puffy, white clouds that stood dominion over the Atchafalaya Basin, the intense flames at its base eradicating the last vestiges of its loathsome contents from the Earth. Soon, he thought, the smoldering remains would tumble into the dark waters at its base, descending forever into the vile swamp from which it had arisen.

Nicholas inspected the few items he'd taken along with him in the small boat, hoping that they'd be enough to keep him alive until he made it back to civilization and his uncertain future. Sweat poured off his body, and he knew he reeked of smoke, filth, and the unmistakable stench of death. The detective hoped that the weather in San Diego would be more pleasant.

Twilight descended on the *bayou*, and he found an open area to anchor down and rest for the night. The swamp was alive with the sounds of the thousands of creatures that called it home, a symphony of endless beauty to his tired ears. The detective huddled up as comfortably as he could manage and looked up into the stars overhead. He was thirsty, he was hungry, he was tired and alone, but he was alive. Nick never remembered feeling so good.

Before he drifted off to sleep, he thought again about the tragic events that he had witnessed. He mourned the deaths of the Swamp Rats and of Cap'n Guidry, a man he had barely known, but one he would consider one the closest friends he'd ever had. He thought that in many ways, Guidry had become like a father to him, a father that he had never known, but searched for his entire life.

The thought brought back the image of the sad, deformed creature in the attic, holding the picture of Lillian St. Pierre, of another lost child that had searched in vain for the

BILLY

love of its parent. Nick buried the unpleasant recollection at once. He didn't want to see those images in his mind ever again. Fatigue won its battle against Nick's restlessness and painful memories, and he drifted off to sleep.

Even in slumber, he found he could not escape the horrors of the Atchafalaya. For a long time after his escape from the desolate wilderness, he was haunted by the things he had encountered. The feelings of dread invaded his dreams, the suppressed memories of sharp claws and jagged teeth filled his nights. In his nightmares, he smelled the sickening odor of death and heard the cries of dying men and the terrifying, victorious roar of the beast.

Over time, most of these images faded, but never truly disappeared. Unfortunately for the traumatized detective, other more disturbing images refused to go away. He often woke up in the middle of the night, covered in sweat and breathing hard, and wondered if his night terrors ever disturbed Marie. At those times, he would stare at the ceiling in the dark, trying to calm down and slow his beating heart, hoping to drift off to a slumber devoid of the demons of the past.

Frequently, in those silent moments, he would think about his visit to St. Elizabeth's to see Margaret Evans. He knew at those moments, wherever she was, that frightened little girl saw the same image in her head that haunted Nick. She had realized the true horror of the monster in the swamp, but was unable to come to terms with it and retreated to a prison in her mind.

Nick refused to let it overtake him, refused to give in. Instead, he lumbered on and tried to forget the unforgettable, a task he was unable to fully accomplish. Nicholas Vizier was never able to forget the horror of the smiling boy in the attic, or of the monsters that killed him.

THE END

GLOSSARY

BAYOU a slow moving river
BAYOU NOIR black slow moving river
BEBETTE a little monster
"BECK MOI TCHEW!" "Bite my ass!"
BIOQUE moron
BON RIEN a good for nothing or lazy man
BONNE A RIENNE a good for nothing or promiscuous woman
BOO a term of endearment, such as sweetie, or darling
BOSCOYO cypress knee
BOUG boy
BRACQUE crazy
"CA VIENS?" "How's it coming?"
CAIMON alligator
CAPON coward
CHER a term of endearment
"CHO! CO!" "Wow!"
"CO FAIRE?" "Why?"
COONASS ethnic term for Cajun; sometimes considered derogatory, sometimes used with pride
"COO-WEE!" "Wow! Look at that!"
COUYON an ignorant person
DEFANTE' a dear departed sainted woman

GLOSSARY

"DIT MON LA VERITE'!" "Tell me the truth!"; a response when told something unbelievable
"EMBRASSE MOI TCHEUE!" "Kiss my ass!"
EN D'OEUILLE to be in mourning
FAIBLESSE faint
"FAIT PAS UNE ESQUANDAL!" "Don't make so much noise!"
"FEET PUE TAN!" "You goddamn son of a bitch!"
"FILS DE PUTAIN" or *"FILS DE PUTE"* "Son of a bitch."
FREESONS goose bumps
FREMEERS grossed out
"GA-LEE!" term of excitement
GRAND big
GRAND BEEDE big, clumsy man
GUMBO a thick highly seasoned soup
JE VAS TE PASSE UNE CALOTTE to threaten to slap someone
"MAIS, JAMAIS D' LA VIE!" "Well, never in my life!"
MAKE THE MISERE' to cause trouble or misery
MAL AU COUER need to throw up
MAL PRIS stuck in a bad way
"MAUDIT" "Goddamn!"

GLOSSARY

"MERCI BEAUCOUP" "Thank you very much"
MERDE' slang for human excrement
MOTIER FOUX half crazy
"OO YE YI!" "That hurts!" or "I am sad!"
PAPA NOEL Santa Clause
PAPERE grandpa
PARRAN godfather
PARESSE lazy
PAUVRE poor
PEESHWANK little girl
"PIC KEE MOI!" "Fuck me!"
"PIC KEE TOI!" "Fuck you!"
PIROGUE small, flat bottomed boat
PODNA partner
POSSEDE' possessed; term for a bad, mischievous child
P'TIT BOUG little boy
"QUE C'EST Q' CA?" "What is that?"
RACONTEUR a storyteller
SKINNY MULLET a skinny person
"TUAT T'EN GROSSE BUECHE!" "You have a big mouth!"
VIEUX elderly man
"VOILA MERDE'" "Go to shit."
ZEERAHB disgusting

ACKNOWLEDGEMENTS

The author wishes to thank all of the people who have read my books and encouraged me to write more. Special thanks go out to my family who live with my insanity on a daily basis.

THANK YOU

Thank you for reading my book, "Billy". I hope you enjoyed reading it as much as I did writing it.

As you are probably aware, new independent self-published authors, like myself, have a tough time getting reviews. Reviews are absolutely essential in providing important feedback to me as a writer, and a recommendation for potential new readers.

I would really appreciate it if you would share your opinion via an honest review at Amazon.

ABOUT THE AUTHOR

Clayton E. Spriggs lives in Southeast Louisiana where he enjoys all the fine food, loyal friendship, and quality football a man could desire. This is his second novel.

Clayton E. Spriggs can be contacted at

cespriggs@pennmillpub.com

OTHER BOOKS
By

Clayton E. Spriggs

Johnson Road
The Saga Begins

Peterson County Murders
**Book Two of the
Johnson Road Saga**

The Bone Puzzle
Stallworth's First Big Case

JOHNSON ROAD
The Saga Begins

Hiding in plain sight, a predator stalks its prey.

When Purvis Johnson fell on hard times, he agreed to sell most of his land to a real estate developer. Before long, the dirt road that once served as his makeshift driveway became a paved street. Newly constructed houses sprung up on both sides. Families moved in. The quiet neighborhood became the perfect place to raise a family

Meet Jake and Mary Bickman and their two sons, the first to move into their new home. Soon, Thomas and Gladys Jenkins buy the house across the street and introduce a beautiful baby girl to the world. The wealthy Peterson couple and their two children build the big house near the end of the block, right next door to the tiny shack where the Johnsons still reside. One by one, tragedy will strike them all.

Welcome to Peterson County, Alabama, mid-twentieth century Americana; a quaint, rural community on its journey to becoming the suburban utopia promised by the American Dream. By the time the dreamers realize they are trapped inside a nightmare, it's too late. Something has gone terribly wrong inside the dream – something evil – something on Johnson Road.

PETERSON COUNTY MURDERS

Book Two of the Johnson Road Saga

Chasing A Serial Killer

From the moment they found the body, the hunt was on.

Now that the FBI and US Marshalls were involved, Sheriff Clifford Gaskin and Deputy Sean Willis were confident it was only a matter of time before they tracked down the murderer and brought justice to the people of Peterson County.

Detective Robert Stallworth wasn't so sure. This was no ordinary criminal they were searching for. This killer was clever and cruel, but most of all, he was evil. Only hell itself could have produced such a monster, and this demon wasn't going to stop. He was having too much fun. Only the detective and the killer knew what this psychopath was capable of and what really happened on Johnson Road.

Coming Soon

The third novel in the Johnson Road Saga

Detective Robert Stallworth searches for the monster that preys on his unsuspecting victims with impunity, but how can he find a man that no one believes exists? The seasoned detective is capable and relentless in his pursuit, determined to bring the criminal to justice. He'll find him if it's the last thing he does. The killer is counting on it.

THE BONE PUZZLE

When a severed foot is discovered in the Dead River Swamp, Detective Robert Stallworth, known for his special talent for finding dead things, is called in to look for the rest of the body. But his job gets even harder when parts of more than one body turn up. Follow the detective as he puts the pieces together to find out who the victims were, where they came from, how they ended up in the swamp, and, most importantly, who put them there.

PART ONE: HOCUS POCUS
Illusions can be deadly

PART TWO: HALLELUJAH
The swamp will keep our secrets

PART THREE: THE HOLY RELIC
Foot bone connected to the heel bone

PART FOUR: REVELATION
Beware of false prophets

PART FIVE: RETRIBUTION
There was only one way out

PART SIX: REDEMPTION
Let the games begin

PART SEVEN: RESURRECTION
When a prophet stands trial,
expect a miracle

Buy *The Bone Puzzle* today and find out how Detective Robert Stallworth uncovers the shocking truth and finds justice for the innocent victims.

FREE BOOKS

Sign up for Clayton E. Spriggs VIP Mail and receive info on how to get FREE eBOOKS and special offers on new releases. Of course, you will be able to unsubscribe at any time. Thank You.

pennmillpub.com/vipmail-CES

Made in the USA
Columbia, SC
29 September 2024